For my brothers,
Robert, Nigel and Michael Tanner,
with love

CONTENTS

CONTENTS

The ancient tale of Frisia, crown princess of Merne, is a curious one. There was a time when people knew it only as a children's story. Now, of course, it is famous, because it played such an important part in the life of Goldie Roth, Fifth Keeper of the Museum of Dunt.

Frisia was a warrior princess, a brilliant archer and swordswoman and a natural leader. She lived in what was, at the time, one of the most dangerous places in the world – the royal court of Merne.

In those days, the court was full of plots and vicious intrigues. At the centre of most of them was the king's physician, an ambitious woman who was secretly in the pay of Graf von Nagel, the rebel warlord. This physician, helped by members of the royal guard, carried out several assassination attempts on Frisia and her father the king.

Frisia survived these plots to lead a tiny army against von Nagel and his followers. The result of the ensuing battle has never been clear. Some say that von Nagel was defeated, and died with Frisia's sword through his heart. Others say that it was the princess who died, and that her body was carried away by the beasts of the field, who had risen up to fight beside her.

No one knows what happened to the physician.

A MESSAGE FROM THE MUSEUM

The scream woke Goldie Roth from a deep sleep. She sat bolt upright, thinking for a moment that she was back in the terrible events of six months ago, with the city of Jewel on the brink of invasion and her friend Toadspit about to be murdered in front of her eyes.

Then she heard Ma's quiet voice in the next room, and she knew that Pa had had another nightmare. She slipped out of bed, threw a dressing gown over her shoulders and hurried into her parents' room. 'Pa?' she said. 'Are you all right?'

Goldie Roth

Pa smiled weakly up at her from a knot of bedclothes. 'Sorry to wake you, sweeting,' he mumbled.

'Your father had a bad dream,' said Ma. 'But it's gone now.' And she too smiled, though her knuckles were white and her fingers trembled.

It pierced Goldie to the heart to see them trying to pretend that nothing was wrong. She unknotted the bedclothes and tucked them around Pa's shoulders, wishing there was something more she could do.

'Were you dreaming about the House of Repentance again?' she said.

Pa flinched. He and Ma glanced at each other, and a world of pain and sorrow passed between them.

It was a little more than ten months since the two of them had been thrown into the dungeons of the House of Repentance. They had never told Goldie what had happened to them there, but she could see the scars that were left behind.

Pa had dreadful nightmares. Ma had a cough that sounded as if it would tear her lungs out. They were both too thin and, even now, long after their release, they had an exhausted look about them, as if something was gnawing at them from the inside.

Goldie wished that they would talk to her about it. But they never did. Instead, they sighed and changed the subject.

'A— A message came for you today, sweeting,' said Pa, struggling to sit up. 'Where did I put it? It was from the Museum of Dunt.'

This time it was Goldie who flinched, although she hid it so well that her father didn't notice. Memories flooded through her. *Toadspit – his whole body plastered in mud – turned towards her and laughed. A warm canine tongue swept across her face, and a deep voice rumbled, 'You are as brave as a brizzlehound—'*

With an effort, she dragged herself back to the present. Pa was fumbling for a scrap of paper that lay on the table beside the bed. 'Here it is.' His forehead creased. 'It's from Herro Dan and Olga Ciavolga. It seems that they want you to be the museum's Fifth Keeper!'

Fifth Keeper of the Museum of Dunt . . . The familiar longing welled up inside Goldie so suddenly and so strongly that she could hardly breathe.

She said nothing, but Pa must have seen some echo of it on her face. 'Do you— Do you *want* to be Fifth Keeper, sweeting? Because—'

'Because if you do,' interrupted Ma, 'we wouldn't stop you.'

'We wouldn't dream of stopping you!'

'It's just—'

'It's just that it's such a big responsibility,' said Pa.

3

'We're worried that it might be too much for you.'

'And—' Ma gripped Goldie's hand. 'And you'd have to be away from home such a lot.' She began to cough.

Goldie patted her gently on the back and tried not to think about the Museum of Dunt, and how much – how *very* much – she wanted to be Fifth Keeper.

'Of course,' said Pa, chewing his lip, 'it's possible that Herro Dan and Olga Ciavolga really need your help. If they do—'

'If they *need* you, then you mustn't hesitate,' said Ma. She tried to let go of Goldie's hand, but didn't quite manage. 'Your father and I talked about this earlier.'

'We did,' said Pa. 'And we both agreed. If they need you, you must go!'

Goldie could hardly bear it. They were doing their best to be fair, but she could see how much they hated the thought of her being away from home for even a little while.

And so she forced every scrap of longing out of her voice and said, 'They don't *really* need me. They've got Sinew and Toadspit to help them.'

Pa frowned, wanting to believe her. 'Are you sure?'

'You're not staying home because of us, are you?' said Ma, still clutching her hand. 'You mustn't do that. We want you to be happy.'

A warm canine tongue swept across her face—

Goldie smiled. 'I *am* happy,' she said. And because she was a trained liar, she sounded as if she meant it.

She sat with her parents until they drifted off to sleep again. Then she tiptoed back to her room, pulled on her smock, woollen stockings and jacket, and slipped out the front door.

Ten months was not such a long time really. But to Goldie – hurrying through the silent Old Quarter towards Toadspit's house – it felt like a lifetime. Ten months ago she had worn a silver guardchain that tied her to her parents or to one of the Blessed Guardians. She had never been anywhere alone, and was almost as helpless as an infant.

But then she ran away and took refuge in the Museum of Dunt. And in the months that she spent there, she grew up. More than that, she became an accomplished thief and a skilled liar. She learned the Three Methods of Concealment, and the First Song, and how to act with a steely courage, even when she was almost overwhelmed with fear.

The lessons fed some deep need inside her, and the museum quickly came to feel like home. The only thing missing was Ma and Pa. *They* were locked up in the

House of Repentance, imprisoned by the Fugleman, the leader of the Blessed Guardians.

And why were they imprisoned?

Goldie turned the corner onto Gunboat Canal. 'Because of me,' she whispered.

In the Jewel of ten months ago, running away was a crime. The Fugleman could not get his hands on Goldie, but it was the easiest thing in the world to pluck Ma and Pa from their bed and drag them before the Court of the Seven Blessings. There they were tried and sentenced for being the parents of a criminal child.

It was my fault, thought Goldie. *Everything that happened to them was my fault.*

It had rained earlier in the night, and the footpaths of Gunboat Canal were slick with mud. Goldie stopped outside Toadspit's house, took a deep breath, and threw a pebble at the window above her head. Then she slipped back into the shadows and waited.

She had lied when she told her parents that the Museum of Dunt didn't need her. The museum *did* need her, to help guard the dangerous secrets that lay within its walls.

But Ma and Pa needed her too, and she could not leave them.

She wrapped her fingers around the enamel brooch that she wore on her collar – the brooch that had once belonged to her long-lost Auntie Praise. But the little blue bird with its outstretched wings brought her no comfort.

Pa thought that there had only been one message from the Museum of Dunt. He was wrong. In the last few months Goldie had had more than a dozen messages, each one asking when she was going to take up her position as Fifth Keeper.

Tonight she would reply.

Never.

THE CHILD-STEALERS

'*Never?*' said Toadspit, in tones of utter disbelief.

Goldie swallowed. She had known that this would be hard, but it was even worse than she had expected. 'No. Never.'

As she spoke she felt a prickle between her shoulder blades. She glanced back and saw a small figure duck out of sight. Someone was following them.

Toadspit hadn't noticed. 'But you *want* to be Fifth Keeper,' he said. 'I *know* you do!'

Bonnie

'Yes, but—'

'So what's stopping you?'

'I told you! Ma and Pa—'

Toadspit interrupted her. 'Apart from me, there hasn't been a new keeper for a couple of hundred years! How can you just throw away an invitation like that?'

'I'm *not* just throwing it away—'

'Yes you are! Look at this!' Toadspit waved his left arm in front of her. 'No cuff, no guardchain! We got rid of them! We're supposed to be free, but now you—' He broke off, glaring at her in disgust. 'This is so stupid!'

Stung, Goldie glared back at him. 'You don't understand!'

Toadspit's face closed in a scowl, and Goldie wondered why she had bothered to wake him up. She hadn't seen him for months, and she had forgotten how annoying he could be. She should have gone straight to the museum.

In the back of her mind a little voice whispered, *But he is right. You were born to be Fifth Keeper. It is your destiny.*

Goldie ignored it, just as she ignored Toadspit. She couldn't leave Ma and Pa, and that was the end of it.

The two children continued on their way in angry silence. Goldie saw no one on the streets – except for the shadowy figure that still crept in their wake.

9

But as they crossed Old Arsenal Bridge and began to climb the hill towards the museum, the quietness was broken by heavy footsteps stamping down the road towards them. Goldie hesitated, suddenly uneasy. There was something threatening about those footsteps, and if she had been by herself, she would have slipped into the nearest doorway until whoever it was had passed.

But Toadspit's scowl was like a challenge.

He expects me to hide, she realised. And she stuck her nose in the air and kept walking.

The footsteps grew louder. Nailed boots struck the cobblestones. By the light of the watergas lamps, Goldie saw two men in long oilskin coats swaggering down the middle of the road. One of them was a huge slab of a fellow with ragged blond hair. The other was smaller, but his face was as sharp as a fishhook. As he passed the children, he peered at them, like a butcher inspecting a couple of fat calves.

Fear licked the back of Goldie's neck. But after that first intense look, the sharp-faced man seemed to lose interest. He and his companion strode across the bridge and disappeared into the darkness.

Toadspit scowled even harder. Goldie's fear turned to irritation. She spun around and called, 'You can come out now, Bonnie.'

There was a hiccup of surprise from the direction

of the bridge, then a small girl with dark hair stepped into the lamplight. The hem of her nightdress showed beneath her smock, and in her hand was an old-fashioned longbow and a quiver of arrows.

Toadspit stared at his little sister. 'What are *you* doing here?'

Bonnie's chin went up. 'I'm going to the museum with you. I followed you all the way from home and you didn't even notice.'

'Of course I did.'

'No you didn't, or you would've sent me back.' Bonnie grinned. 'Goldie almost saw me once. But I hid just in time.'

'Near the terminus,' said Goldie. 'When you slipped.'

Bonnie's face fell. Toadspit turned his look of disgust on Goldie. 'You knew she was following us and you didn't tell me?'

Goldie shrugged, still angry with him. 'She's not going to come to any harm, not with us here.'

'I'd be all right even if I was by myself,' said Bonnie. She held up the bow. 'I'm armed.'

'You'd probably shoot yourself in the foot,' said Toadspit. 'Where did you get that thing?'

'Olga Ciavolga gave it to me. She said I had a talent for it. She said I could be a champion archer one day, like Princess Frisia.'

Toadspit looked blank.

'You know, the warrior princess of Merne,' said Bonnie. 'There's a painting of her in the museum. She lived five hundred years ago and she was really brave. Some assassins tried to kill her father the king with poisoned air, and she saved him. And she was the best archer anyone had ever seen. I'm going to be just like her. I've been practising.'

Toadspit rolled his eyes. 'You're a pest, Bonnie. I bet you woke Ma and Pa up when you left.'

'I didn't!'

'We're going to have to take you home—'

'We haven't got time,' interrupted Goldie. 'We have to get to the museum.'

'And if we meet any enemies on the way,' said Bonnie, 'I can shoot them.'

Toadspit snorted. 'I bet you couldn't even hit the side of a house.'

'I could. I could hit—' Bonnie looked around. 'I could hit that wooden pole. The one with the gas lamp, on the other side of the bridge. Will you let me come with you if I do?'

'No—'

'Yes,' said Goldie. 'If you hit it you can come with us.'

Toadspit bared his teeth. 'Looks like you'll be going home then, doesn't it, Bonniekins.'

His sister smirked. 'You only call me that when you think you're going to lose.'

'Stop it, you two,' said Goldie. 'Bonnie, get on with it.'

Bonnie took an arrow from her quiver, fitted it carefully to her bow and turned so that she was standing side-on to the gas lamp, with her legs apart and the tail end of the arrow slotted between her fingers. She drew her right arm back until her hand rested against her cheek. She raised the bow, then lowered it a little.

There was a moment of complete stillness. Then her fingers twitched, the bowstring made a *thunking* sound, and the arrow flew across the bridge and planted itself firmly in the pole. Bonnie gave a little *Hmm* of satisfaction and lowered the bow.

Toadspit stared. 'It was a fluke.'

'You want me to do it again? I can, ten times in a row.'

'No,' said Goldie quickly. 'It's all right, you can come with us.'

'Hang on, I've got to get my arrow,' said Bonnie and, before Goldie could stop her, she ran back across the bridge.

Toadspit took a step after her. 'I'm going to take her home.'

'You can't,' said Goldie. 'You agreed.'

'No. *You* agreed. *I* never said she could come with us.'

'Don't be so stubborn. You know she'll be all right.'

'Will she?' Toadspit's voice rose angrily. 'I'm glad *you're* so sure. But then you're not responsible for her, are you.'

'No, but—'

'Well, I am. And *I* say she goes home.' He shouted over his shoulder. 'Did you hear that, Bonnie? You're going home.'

'But *why*?' By now, Goldie was shouting too, with frustration. She could see the night trickling away. At this rate she wouldn't get anywhere near the museum, which meant she would have to leave her parents alone *again*, tomorrow night or the night after.

'Because she's too little,' said Toadspit. 'She's only ten.'

Goldie shook her head in disbelief. 'You're just trying to make things happen *your* way as usual. Well, don't expect me to hang around while you take her home.'

'Who asked you to hang around? Not me.'

'Good, I'm going then.'

'Good!'

They glared at each other for a moment longer, then Goldie turned and stamped off up the hill. Behind her a stone rattled across the road, as if someone had kicked it.

14

Ha! thought Goldie. If he was in a temper now, he'd be in a worse one soon. She slowed down a little, and waited for Bonnie's protests to begin.

But it was Toadspit's voice she heard, as brittle as glass on the night air. 'G-Goldie?'

She spun around. Toadspit was standing on the far side of the bridge, staring at something on the ground.

The night grew suddenly colder. With a sick feeling in her stomach, Goldie raced down the hill and across the bridge. And there, in the stark light of the gas lamp, she saw what Toadspit was staring at.

In the middle of the road, Bonnie's longbow lay abandoned. The quiver had been tossed to one side and arrows were scattered around it like fallen wheat. One of them was stained with blood.

There was no sign of Bonnie.

15

To the Docks

Toadspit was so pale that Goldie thought he was going to faint. Her own skin felt like ice, and she had to force herself to scan the ground around that terrible arrow.

'I— I don't think the blood is Bonnie's,' she whispered. She pointed to the tell-tale marks in the mud. 'There were two men. See their bootprints where they ran towards her? They took her by surprise. Look at the way her prints are scuffed.'

She broke off, remembering the men who had swaggered past them. They must have doubled back and seen Bonnie come out of

Toadspit

hiding. They must have waited until she was close enough to grab – while Goldie and Toadspit, who were supposed to be looking after her, shouted at each other.

She swallowed, and studied the ground again. 'I— I think she stabbed one of them with the arrow. It's *his* blood. And look, one of them has picked her up. You can see where *her* footprints stop, and *his* get deeper, as if he's carrying something. Here, they went this way.'

Their argument forgotten, they set out to track the two men through the dark city. To Goldie's relief, Toadspit was steady on his feet again, but he clutched the bow in his fist, and there was a grimness about him that she had never seen before.

They lost the bootprints many times. For all their skill, they could only track what they could see, and the light from the moon and the watergas lamps was never enough. Sometimes the prints disappeared altogether, and they had to search in every direction until they found a fresh smear of mud, or a pebble kicked out of place.

It was all too easy to make a mistake. Once they followed the wrong person for nearly three blocks and had to backtrack quickly. After that, Goldie borrowed Toadspit's folding knife and cut notches in a stick to show how long and how wide the bootprints were, so they wouldn't be misled again.

The children tracked the two men past the space where the Great Hall used to be, past the indoor markets and past the grey stone carcass of the House of Repentance. At last they saw warehouses looming out of the darkness, and the newly-repaired iron levees that protected Jewel from the sea. Rising above the levees were the masts of ships.

'The docks,' Goldie whispered. It was the first time she had spoken for more than half an hour, and her voice sounded strange in her ears.

The bootprints led the children to an old wooden wharf, where fishing boats were moored nose to tail, with their nets strung out to dry and lobster pots piled high on their decks. A mist was rolling in from the south. The stink of seaweed and fish hung over everything.

Goldie could hear the water lapping against the piles beneath her, and the slow creak of wooden hulls. Somewhere, a chain rattled. A grey spotted cat darted across her path like a puff of smoke. The chain rattled again, very close this time.

There was a hiss of gas, and an engine struggled to life.

The children shrank back into the shadows, peering at the boat opposite. It was small and stumpy, with a single mast and a deckhouse at the back. A coarse rope net hung over its side. Its engine belched uncertainly, then steadied.

Toadspit's fingers dug into Goldie's flesh. 'It's them,' he hissed. 'It must be.'

As he spoke, the engine took on a deeper note. The water swirled and slapped against the wooden piles. The mast trembled, and the boat began to edge away from the wharf.

There was no time to wonder if it really *was* the right boat. Goldie and Toadspit raced across the wharf and threw themselves over the widening gap. It was a long jump and Goldie almost didn't make it. Her fingers touched the rope net. Missed. Touched again. Her right hand fumbled. Her left hand clung desperately. Her feet flailed in mid-air—

Then, just when she thought she must fall and be swallowed up by the cold, churning water, her toes found the net. She clutched at it, pressing her whole body against the side of the boat and gasping for breath.

Beside her, Toadspit was already crawling upwards. Goldie scrambled after him, and the two of them slipped over the rail and sank down behind the deckhouse, with Bonnie's bow between them.

Somewhere nearby a man cried, 'Half speed!' The boat surged, and the lights of Jewel disappeared into the mist. Ahead, everything was darkness.

RETURN OF
A TRAITOR

The Fugleman

The Grand Protector of Jewel was at her desk when the note from Vice-Marshal Amsel arrived. She pushed her papers and her early morning cup of hot chocolate to one side, adjusted her eyeglasses and read the hastily scribbled message.

'You're joking!' The words burst out of her before she could stop them.

'It's no joke, Your Grace,' said the corporal of militia who had brought the note. 'The prisoner walked up to the Eastern Gate an hour ago. Looked as if he'd been living rough for a while.'

The Protector gulped a mouthful of hot chocolate and re-read the note, her pulse beating an angry tattoo. 'He gave himself up? He wasn't captured?'

The corporal shook his head.

'Well,' said the Protector. 'I suppose I must see him. Tell the vice-marshal to send him to me.'

As soon as the corporal had gone, she took her gold chain and stiff crimson robe from the corner closet and put them on. Then she sat down to await the arrival of the worst traitor the city had ever known. The man who had plotted to enslave its citizens and set himself up as dictator. The man whom everyone had assumed to be dead, lost in the Great Storm.

Her younger brother. The Fugleman of Jewel.

The Protector almost laughed when they brought the prisoner in. He wore so many chains that he clanked like an iron foundry. She leaned back in her chair and studied him.

He was thinner than the last time she'd seen him, and everything about him was ragged and filthy. His hair was still black, of course, and he had a certain handsomeness beneath the grime. But his shoulders were slumped and his eyes were fixed on the floor. The fine proud Fugleman of six months ago had disappeared completely.

At the memory of that terrible time, when the city had come so close to disaster, the Protector felt all temptation to laugh vanish. 'Wait outside,' she said to the militiamen.

The guards backed out the door. There was silence in the office. The Protector steepled her fingers, trying to control her anger. 'Well, Herro?' she said. (She would *not* call him brother. The word would stick in her throat.) 'What do you have to say for yourself?'

'May I— May I sit down?' The Fugleman's voice – his glorious voice that had once swayed crowds – was so weak and hoarse that he sounded like an old man.

'*Last* time you were here,' said the Protector grimly, 'you did not bother to ask. You put your feet up on my desk as if this office was a common beerhouse.' She bared her teeth in a humourless smile. 'Perhaps you recall the occasion? It was just before you had me imprisoned in the House of Repentance.'

The Fugleman swallowed. 'You are right to remind me, sist—'

'*Don't* call me that!'

'I beg your pardon.' He bowed his head. 'The truth is,

I am a broken man – Your Grace. Broken on the rocks of my own foolish ambition. I am deeply sorry for the crimes I committed.'

'Is that *it*? You're *sorry*? You try to sell the city into slavery, and all you can say is—' The Protector broke off, biting down on her fury and wishing whole-heartedly that the Fugleman had not chosen this particular moment to return from the dead.

The last six months had not been easy for the people of Jewel. So much had changed in such a short time. The Blessed Guardians had been put on trial and cast out of the city. The House of Repentance had been boarded up. The silver guardchains that children wore to keep them safe were banned, and the heavy brass punishment chains vanished as if they had never existed.

At first, unable to get used to the new freedoms, many parents simply tied their sons and daughters up with lengths of rope, or followed them whenever they left the house, ducking around corners so as not to be discovered.

Gradually, however, they grew bolder. The ropes disappeared. Some families bought cats or dogs. Birds returned to the city. For the first time in her life, the Protector heard the sound of children laughing as they played in the street.

But then, just three weeks ago, a boy had broken his

leg. Six days later, a girl fell into Dead Horse Canal and nearly drowned. The accidents shocked everyone. The Protector had begun to hear mutterings. *This would never have happened under the Blessed Guardians.*

And now the Fugleman, the leader of the Guardians, was back. The Protector wished she could see inside his head. She knew that he was a superb actor. Was he acting now? Was he as humbled as he seemed to be, or was it a trick? She rapped her fingernail on the desk.

Outside the window a dog began to howl. At the same time, someone knocked on the door of her office. 'Sorry to interrupt, Your Grace,' said one of the militiamen, poking his head in, 'but there's a messenger from the Museum of Dunt. Name of Sinew. He said it was—'

'Urgent!' A tall, awkward-looking man in a long black cloak and a red woollen scarf pushed past him. 'They've gone, Protector, vanished overnight—'

He saw the Fugleman and his mouth snapped shut – then, quicker than a thought, split open again in a foolish grin. He threw his arms wide. 'Yes, my worries have vanished overnight,' he proclaimed, 'because the *Fugleman* has returned! And I am filled with joy!'

He grabbed the Fugleman by the shoulders and kissed him soundly on both cheeks. The Protector's mouth fell open in astonishment, and she was about to protest. But then she saw the uprush of blood in the Fugleman's face, and she pinned her lips together, sat back in her chair and waited to see what would happen next.

Sinew draped his arm around the prisoner's shoulders. 'So,' he burbled cheerfully, 'where on *earth* have you been? The Protector here was convinced you were dead, but I said, "No, he's just wandered off to do his murdering and looting somewhere else for a change. He'll be back, never fear, like a bad smell."' He wrinkled his long nose. 'Speaking of bad smells . . .'

A pulse throbbed in the Fugleman's temple, but he stared at the floor and said nothing. Outside the building, the howling went on and on.

The Protector stood up and unlatched the window. Sitting on the footpath below her was a little white dog with a curly tail and one black ear. Its head was tipped back and its eyes closed. Its muzzle pointed to the sky.

'Arooo-oooooo-ooooooooooh,' it howled. 'Arrrooo-oooooooooo-ooooooooooooooh.'

'Isn't that the – um – dog from the museum?' said the Protector. It was hard to make herself heard above the pitiful sound. 'What's the matter with him?'

'Oh, nothing serious,' said Sinew. 'He's got fleas, that's all, and wants the world to know about it.' He nudged the Fugleman. 'Terrible things, fleas. Can't stand them myself. Ooh look, there's one now.'

Quick as a flash, his hand burrowed into the

Fugleman's matted hair. The Fugleman jerked away as if he had been burned, his face livid with anger.

Sinew didn't seem to notice. He held something up between his fingernails. 'Got it,' he declared, with a satisfied smile. 'And now we crush it—' his nails clicked together '—like the nasty little parasite it is.'

The Protector had seen enough. She pulled the window closed and turned to the waiting militiaman. 'Tell Vice-Marshal Amsel that the Fugleman – the *ex*-Fugleman – is to be taken to the House of Repentance.'

'But it's boarded up, Your Grace.'

'Then unboard it. I want him guarded around the clock.'

The militiaman grabbed the Fugleman's arm. 'Come on, you.'

As the door closed behind them, Sinew's foolishness fell away like a discarded coat. 'Your Grace,' he said in a low voice. 'Do you remember Goldie Roth and Toadspit Hahn?'

'What? Who?' said the Protector, who was still thinking about the Fugleman. Then her mind cleared and she said, 'Yes, of course. Such brave children. If it wasn't for them, *he*—' she grimaced at the door '—would have succeeded in his vicious plans.'

'They have disappeared, along with Toadspit's sister Bonnie.'

'*Disappeared?*' The Protector rubbed her forehead, trying to take in the news. 'Is that why the dog— I mean, the brizzlehound. I did not want to say so in front of the Fugleman, but that creature outside my window *is* a brizzlehound, is it not? Broo?'

Sinew nodded grimly. 'Goldie's father, Herro Roth, came to us at first light, very distressed because his daughter was missing. Broo and I went back with him and tracked Goldie's movements. It seems she slipped out of the house in the middle of the night and went to the Hahns' place to pick up Toadspit. We think Bonnie followed them. They appeared to be heading towards the museum, but along the way Bonnie was abducted. Toadspit and Goldie went after the men who took her.'

The Protector sat down very suddenly. 'Slavers?'

'Maybe.'

'I have heard that Old Lady Skint and her crew are growing active again. It could be them.' The Protector's brow furrowed. 'Or maybe someone taking a child for ransom? There's an army of mercenaries in the Southern Archipelago that has been snatching travellers off the road and selling them back to their families. Perhaps those mercenaries have brought their crimes north to Jewel.'

'Whoever it was,' said Sinew, 'we tracked them to the docks, and there we lost them. Four ships left overnight

– the *Fighting Dove*, the *Black Bob*, the *Jumping at Shadows* and the *Ungrateful Child*.' His mouth tightened. 'I have no idea which one they might be on.'

With a shudder, the Protector picked up her pen and dipped it in the inkpot. 'I'll get those ships traced immediately, and send out names and descriptions of the children.'

'Descriptions, yes,' said Sinew. 'But let us keep their names to ourselves for now. I will ask their parents to do the same.'

The Protector nodded towards the door. 'Because of our prisoner?'

'Yes. He has good reason to hate Goldie and Toadspit. I know he'll be locked up, but still— The less he knows, the better.'

'He claims to be humble and repentant.'

'Does he indeed?' said Sinew. 'Perhaps he is repentant, I cannot tell. But humble? No. The overwhelming pride is still there, just below the surface. I would watch him if I were you. I would watch him very carefully indeed.'

He touched his finger to his brow in an informal salute, and was gone. Outside the window, Broo howled as if it was the end of the world.

THE *PIGLET*

oldie was so cold and stiff that she could hardly move. The end of Bonnie's bow poked into her ribs, and the salty air had stuck her eyelids together. She thought that she had slept a little, but she wasn't sure.

She and Toadspit had found this hiding place last night – a tarpaulin-covered dinghy, halfway along the deck of the fishing boat.

Smudge and Cord

Now the edges of the tarpaulin let in a glimmer of daylight. It was morning.

Goldie licked her dry lips. Ma and Pa would have woken up by now, and found her gone. Her heart ached at the thought. How would they manage without her? What if her disappearance made Pa's nightmares worse? What if Ma's cough turned into a fever?

Beside her, Toadspit lifted the edge of the tarpaulin, just far enough to see out. Goldie squirmed up to the gap and peered through it, grateful for the distraction.

The deck of the boat was covered with nets and barrels and ropes, and a pile of glass floats like huge green bubbles. In the stern, the sharp-faced man from the night before was standing beneath an open-fronted deckhouse. His legs were braced and he held a heavy upright pole that moved back and forth with the movement of the sea. His oilskin coat flapped in the wind.

As Goldie watched, he leaned towards an open hatch and shouted, 'Hey, Smudge.'

A muffled reply came from somewhere below.

'Bring the snotty up,' shouted the sharp-faced man. 'Let's see 'er in daylight.'

Heavy footsteps crossed the lower deck, then a second man, the big one with the blond hair, clambered out of the hatch with Bonnie in his arms and dumped her on the deck next to the mast. Her wrists were tied and there were bruises on her forehead.

In the dinghy, Goldie felt Toadspit tremble with rage.

The big man fumbled behind one of the barrels and pulled out a flat piece of wood. 'Um, Cord?' he said. Despite his enormous size, there was something childlike and eager to please about him. 'You want me to change the name of the boat before someone sees us?'

'Yeah, go on.'

The ship heaved and slapped against the waves. As Cord worked the tiller, the sleeve of his coat fell back, and Goldie saw a bloodstained bandage.

Beneath the tarpaulin, her hands twitched out a message in the silent code of fingertalk. *'That's who Bonnie stabbed with arrow.'*

Toadspit nodded. His eyes flickered back to his sister's bruises.

When Smudge returned, he was carrying a different piece of wood. He held it up for Bonnie to inspect. 'It's a fake name plate, see?' he said, as happily as if she was a friend, rather than a child he had stolen. 'When we was in Jewel we was the *Black Bob*, but now we's the *Piglet*. Ain't that clever? Who's gunna think of lookin' for the good old *Piglet*? No one, that's who.' He grunted with satisfaction. 'It were my idea, weren't it, Cord?' he shouted to the smaller man.

31

Out of the corner of her eye, Goldie saw something move. She nudged Toadspit. The grey spotted cat that had darted across their path on the wharf was slinking around one of the barrels. It was a huge, gaunt, wild-looking creature with torn ears and a bony skull and, when it saw Smudge, it bared its fangs in a silent hiss.

Smudge leaped backwards, an expression of horror on his face. 'Where'd that thing come from? What's it doin' on the *Piglet*?'

'Musta come with us from Spoke.' The sharp-faced man, Cord, sniggered. 'What's the matter, Smudge? You're not scared of that old fleabag, are ya?'

'Course not,' said Smudge quickly. He retreated another step, tucking his fists into his armpits. 'It's just – um – you remember Harrow's fightin' dog? Great big monster of a thing? A coupla months ago he set it onto that cat, for a bit of a laugh. And . . .' He lowered his voice. 'And the cat killed it! I seen it with me own eyes! They reckon – They reckon it's a demon cat! They reckon it can see things that ain't there.'

Cord's snigger turned to a snarl. 'Don't be more of a idjit than ya have to. Find out the snotty's name.'

Without moving, Smudge mumbled, 'Hey, snotty. What's yer name?'

Bonnie sat up very straight. 'My name is – Princess Frisia.' In the dinghy, Toadspit smiled bleakly.

Smudge made a clumsy bow, still keeping an eye on the cat. 'Pleased to meet ya, Princess.'

'Oh, for Bald Thoke's sake!' shouted Cord. 'You're a moron, Smudge. What are ya? A moron. Find out 'er *real* name.'

'That *is* my real name,' said Bonnie. She glared up at Smudge. 'Why did you steal me? My father the king will be very angry.'

Smudge looked confused for a moment. Then Goldie saw a cunning expression slide across his big face. 'We *didn't* steal ya. Yer ma and pa sold ya to us.'

'That's not true!' cried Bonnie.

'Well, course it's not,' said Smudge, sounding surprised at her protest. 'I'm practisin' for the Festival.'

Under the tarpaulin, Toadspit's fingers flashed a message. *What festival?*

Goldie shook her head. *'Don't know.'*

'If she won't tell ya her name,' Cord shouted, 'take 'er below.'

Bonnie pressed herself against the mast. 'I'm not going back down there.'

'You have to,' said Smudge. "E's the boss, so ya gotta do what 'e says.'

'He's not *my* boss,' said Bonnie. 'And *I* like it better up here.'

'Aw, come on, Princess. You'll get me into trouble.' The big man took a step towards her, but the cat hissed at him and he quickly backed away again. 'Um—Cord?'

Cord jerked his head in disgust. 'Do I 'ave to do *everything* meself? Yeah, course I do.' He beckoned furiously to Smudge, who lumbered over to take the tiller.

Beside Goldie, Toadspit gritted his teeth.

Cord was clearly not the least bit afraid of the cat. He marched straight past it, aiming a kick at it on the way. But the cat was not afraid either. It twisted away from the kick and leaped up onto the nearest coil of rope. Its back bristled. Its long claws snaked out and raked Cord's hand.

Cord swore loudly. 'Scratch *me*, would ya? Ya little—!'

'Told ya it was a demon,' shouted Smudge.

'That ain't no demon,' hissed Cord, snatching an iron bar from a nearby barrel. 'And I'll prove it.'

There was a flurry of movement as Bonnie scrambled to her feet and launched herself at him. 'Don't you *dare*!' she cried, kicking his ankles and punching his chest with her bound fists. 'Don't you *dare* hurt that poor cat!'

A chill ran through Goldie. Cord swore again and dropped the iron bar. He grabbed Bonnie by the scruff of the neck, his thin face purple with fury. 'Ya little ratbag,' he snarled. 'It's time ya learned some respect!'

'Careful, boss,' said Smudge uneasily. 'Harrow won't like it if ya damage the goods.'

'Harrow told us to get a snotty, and we did,' growled Cord. 'It's not our fault if she got a bit *mashed up* on the way 'ome!' And he raised his fist.

Goldie had almost stopped breathing. She grasped the edge of the tarpaulin, ready to leap out of the dinghy.

But Toadspit's hands were again flashing in fingertalk. *'Stay here. Need someone they don't know about. Keep this for me!'*

He thrust his folding knife into her pocket. Then he pushed past her and tumbled out onto the deck.

To the two men, it must have seemed as if he had dropped from the sky. He leaped over the barrels and tore his sister away from Cord before the sharp-faced man knew what was happening.

'Toadspit!' cried Bonnie, and she threw her bound hands around her brother's neck.

To Goldie's relief, the sudden appearance of a fourth person shocked Cord out of his mad rage. He leaned back against the rail, breathing heavily. 'Well well, looks like we got *two* snotties, Smudge, instead of one.

We'll 'ave to search the bilges. There might be a whole gaggle of 'em down there, hatchin' out like goslings.' He chortled nastily. 'You and me's gunna be in Harrow's good books.'

'We're not going anywhere with you,' snarled Toadspit.

'I don't see that ya got a choice in the matter,' said Cord. 'Unless ya fancy a *very* long swim.'

He swaggered towards the boy. Goldie sucked in a sharp breath, but Toadspit backed quickly out of reach.

Bonnie stuck her tongue out at Cord. 'You might as well give up now,' she said. 'My brother *kills* people like you.'

'Shush, Bonnie!' hissed Toadspit.

'Bonnie?' said Cord, sarcastically. 'I thought she was some sorta princess.'

Goldie huddled in the dinghy, clutching her bird brooch and shivering with helpless anger. She saw Smudge tie the tiller in place. She watched as he took a brown bottle from his pocket, poured liquid onto a kerchief and crept up behind Toadspit. She caught a whiff of something cloying and strong.

Toadspit must have smelled it at almost the same time, because he let go of Bonnie and whirled around. But he was too slow. Smudge wrapped his big arms around the boy and clamped the kerchief over his nose.

Toadspit struggled and kicked, then went limp.

'What've you *done* to him?' shouted Bonnie, and she attacked Smudge, trying to drag her unconscious brother from his arms. Goldie's muscles ached with the desire to leap out of the dinghy and help, but she did not move.

'Here, gimme that muck, Smudge,' said Cord, grabbing Bonnie from behind. 'I've 'ad enough of snotties. We're gunna keep 'em asleep for the rest of the voyage.'

He held the kerchief over Bonnie's face until she too went limp. Then he handed her to Smudge, who slung both children across his shoulders and carried them below. The cat watched from behind a barrel, its tail whipping from side to side.

Slowly, Goldie let the edge of the tarpaulin fall back into place. A drop of salt water trickled down her forehead, and she wiped it away. She was still shivering, but her anger was beginning to wear off, and she felt stunned by what had just happened.

She was all alone now. No one knew where she was. If Toadspit and Bonnie were to be rescued, she must do it entirely by herself – and the only thing she had to help her was a folding knife.

The thought was almost too much for her. What could she do against a man as violent as Cord? Where were her friends being taken, and why? Who was the mysterious Harrow?

And how will Ma and Pa get on without me?

Something twisted painfully in her chest. She could not turn back, she knew that. She must try to put her parents out of her mind until Toadspit and Bonnie were safe again.

But as the *Piglet* plunged through the waves, heading for an unknown destination, Goldie felt as if a part of her was trying to fly in the opposite direction.

POUNCE

I n a narrow street in one of the
poorer parts of the city of Spoke,
two boys were sitting on a stone
step, watching the shop opposite.
The older boy, Pounce, had his
scabby arms wrapped around
his knees, trying to keep out the
cold wind that was blowing
up from the harbour. He
would have given up ages
ago if it wasn't for the money
that Harrow's underling,
Flense, had promised him.

Pounce

'One thing I'll say about Harrow's mob,' he whispered to the small boy beside him, 'is that they pays well. Not like *most* people. *Most* people try and fob us off with a two-week-old pie that'd 'ave us spewin' in the gutter if we was thick enough to eat it. *And* they expect us to be grateful.'

The younger boy grinned and pushed his white hair out of his eyes. Pounce blew on his cold hands. '*I* reckon they should pay us as much as they pay a grownup,' he said. 'More, prob'ly. Snotties make better spies than grownups. 'Specially street snotties. We's as good as invisible, ain't we, Mousie? We could lie right down in the middle of the Spice Market and die of 'unger, and no one'd notice till our corpses started to stink.'

The white-haired boy pointed to the arm of his jacket, where it sagged under the weight of a dozen sleeping mice.

'Yeah, I s'pose *they'd* notice,' said Pounce. 'Greedy little beggars. They'd prob'ly chew our fingers off before we was even cold.'

Mouse's eyes widened and he laughed in silent delight. Pounce felt a tiny patch of warmth in the pit of his belly. 'Well, anyway, we ain't gunna die of 'unger this week, thanks to Harrow and Flense,' he muttered gruffly.

Mouse pointed to his sleeve again.

'Yeah yeah,' said Pounce. 'And thanks to the sprats.'

He patted the other boy on the arm, careful not to disturb the mice. 'You and them does a good job. There's lotsa times we woulda starved without your fortune-tellin' tricks.'

A line appeared on Mouse's forehead. Pounce held up his hands in mock apology. 'All right, so they's not tricks. They's real. They just *looks* like tricks.'

Across the street, old Warble had been serving behind the counter of his bread shop. Now he came to the door, scratching nervously at one of his hairy eyebrows.

'Here, make out like ya's asleep,' whispered Pounce, dropping his head onto his knees and watching through his fingers.

Beside him, Mouse began to snore gently. But as soon as Warble disappeared back into his shop, the little boy frowned, as if he'd only just realised what they were doing here. He pointed to the shop, then to his own mouth.

'What?' said Pounce, deliberately misunderstanding him. 'You 'ungry?'

Mouse made a wiping gesture, as if to say, Of course he was hungry, he was always hungry, but that wasn't important right now. He pointed to the bread shop again, and smiled and held out his hands. He tapped Pounce's shoulder, then his own.

Pounce sighed. 'Look, Mousie. Ya can't be soft, all

right? I *know* old Warble gives us leftovers when he's got 'em. But that's not the point, see? The point is, Flense is payin' me to keep an eye on 'im.'

Mouse pulled a face and drew his finger across his throat.

'Nah, nothin' like that,' said Pounce quickly. 'No one's gunna get 'urt. Flense is expectin' an important delivery, that's all, and she wants to make sure it arrives safely. She don't trust no one, see. No one except Harrow. It's a wonder she ain't sittin' 'ere 'erself, givin' orders.'

He sniffed, trying to think of some way of distracting Mouse. He didn't usually bring his friend on jobs like this one, but there'd been a lot of rain lately, and he was worried that the old sewer where they lived might flood, or even collapse. He didn't like to leave Mouse there on his own, just in case.

Truth was, Warble might well end up with his throat slit – that was the way things usually ended with Harrow's mob. But it was none of Pounce's business, and none of Mouse's either, however kind the old bread-shop man had been to them. You couldn't be soft, not in this world. Not if you wanted to survive.

'Well now,' he whispered. 'Let's you and me think about what we saw.' He nodded towards the shop door. 'He was nervous, did ya see that? Did ya see how 'e took out 'is snot rag and wiped 'is forehead? As if maybe 'e was expectin' someone, and wasn't real 'appy about it? That's what I'll tell Flense when I report back. Harrow likes details like that. He says they make all the difference, and that's why 'e hires me, 'cos I'm a noticer, and noticers are rare birds.'

To Pounce's relief, Mouse laughed his silent laugh again, and flapped his skinny arms.

'What?' said Pounce, pretending to scowl. 'Ya don't reckon I'm a rare bird?'

Mouse shook his head.

'What am I then? A scrawny old pigeon, with moulty feathers and crusty bits round its eyes? I s'pose yer gunna creep up behind me and whack me with a stick, and roast my corpsie over a fire, like we did to that pigeon the other day.'

Mouse grinned and rubbed his tummy.

For as long as Pounce could remember there hadn't been enough to eat. It was worse in winter, when the cold made your belly stick to your backbone.

'Tell ya what, Mousie,' he said. 'One day I'm gunna find somethin' that Flense and Harrow *really* want. Not just a little spyin' job like this one. Somethin' big and important. Somethin' they'll pay lots and lots of money for. And then, you and me's gunna rent a room. A proper room, with a fireplace. And we's gunna sit by the fire and eat pigeons all day long. Just think of it, eh? The grease runnin' down our chins. Our bellies so fat we can't 'ardly stand up.'

Mouse closed his eyes and licked his lips as if he could already taste the pigeons.

A fierce protectiveness welled up inside Pounce. *I'll do it, too*, he told himself grimly. *I don't care what it is, or who it 'urts, just as long as Harrow'll pay good money for it.*

Aloud he said, 'It's you and me against the world, Mousie. We don't need no one else. You remember that. You stick with your mate Pounce, and he'll get ya all the pigeons you want.'

GOLDIE NO ONE

oldie was dreaming. She knew it was a dream because Blessed Guardian Hope was there, a plump figure in a black cloak and black boxy hat, with the punishment chains coiled like pythons around her waist.

'You're supposed to be dead,' whispered Goldie. 'You died in the Great Storm.'

Guardian Hope smiled and pulled a thin silver chain from the pocket of her robes. She held it up to the light. Then she began to thread it, bit by bit, between Goldie's ribs and around her heart . . .

Goldie No One

Goldie opened her mouth to cry out – and just in time remembered where she was. She bit the inside of her cheek until the dream faded, and leaned back in the narrow doorway. It was almost morning, and all around her the streets of Spoke were waking up.

The *Piglet* had made landfall the night before, after three days at sea. They had been a dreadful three days. From dawn to dusk, Goldie hid in the dinghy, with nothing to eat except some hard biscuits that she found under the seat, along with a sealed jar of water. In the evenings, she watched helplessly as Smudge carried her friends up on deck, fed them, took them to the stinking toilet in the stern, then drugged them again and carried them back below.

At night she slipped out of the dinghy, stretching her aching limbs and wishing that she could steal some of the two men's food. But she dared not do anything that might betray the presence of a *third* child on board the *Piglet*.

When at last they had sailed into Spoke Harbour and Goldie saw its dim outline, looking exactly as it did in the engravings, she could hardly believe it. She had imagined that she and her friends were being carried somewhere so far away and so strange that they would never find their way home again. But here they were, still on the Faroon Peninsula, a few hundred miles down the coast from Jewel!

Her spirits rose. And when Cord and Smudge loaded Toadspit's and Bonnie's limp bodies onto a horse-drawn cart and drove off into the city, she grabbed a useful-looking coil of rope from the deck and followed them.

Although it was late, the footpaths of Spoke were crammed with people. Goldie dodged past them, trying not to lose the cart. Up the narrow streets she went, and away from the harbour, until the smell of the sea was left behind and the houses crowded around her like curious aunts.

The cart stopped halfway up a hill, outside a bread shop. The shop appeared to be closed, but when Cord rapped sharply on the door, a light came on. Goldie caught her breath. Was she about to see the mysterious Harrow?

But whoever came to the door did not show themselves. Instead, Smudge carried the children into the shop, then he and Cord came out and drove away. The door shut behind them. The light went out.

Goldie sank back onto the nearest step and let out the breath she hadn't realised she was holding. Her friends were still unconscious, so she could do nothing tonight except keep watch – and make sure that she was not seen by whoever was in the bread shop.

In the doorway opposite, something moved. Goldie froze, wondering if Harrow had set guards up and down the street. But then she heard a young boy grunt drowsily, and a bare foot slid out and rested on the cobblestones, as limp as old cabbage.

Goldie peered into the shadows. She couldn't see anything much of the boy, except that he was ragged, filthy and fast asleep. In fact, now that she looked more closely, several other doorways were also occupied by sleeping children, some of them alone, some in pairs.

After three days and nights in the *Piglet*'s dinghy, Goldie was nearly as dirty as the boy opposite. She settled back against the door and rested her head on her knees, hoping that anyone who saw her would think she was just another homeless girl, trying to keep out of the wind.

She meant to stay awake. But although she was hungry, and the step beneath her was hard, she was so tired that she fell asleep almost straight away.

She had wild and terrible dreams. Pa crawled up the hill towards her, chased by something that she couldn't bear to look at. Ma wept droplets of blood. Guardian Hope threaded the silver chain through her ribs and around her heart, over and over again.

When Goldie woke up the second time, the street was bustling, the children in the other doorways had disappeared and her stomach was groaning with hunger.

But the dreams lingered, as heavy as stone inside her. *Pa crawled up the hill . . .*

Tears prickled Goldie's eyes and she brushed them away. 'What I need,' she told herself firmly, 'is a plan.'

The first thing she must do was get a sense of the neighbourhood – the back entrances, the dead ends, the directions that danger might come from. Then she must work out how to break into the bread shop. And *then* she must find something to eat.

She paused and, like a faithful dog, her thoughts returned to Ma and Pa. How she *wished* she could go to them, right now! How she wished—

No. She shook her head. She couldn't go home. She *wouldn't* go home, not until she could take Bonnie and Toadspit with her. And that might never happen if she didn't stop worrying about Ma and Pa!

In the back of her mind, a little voice whispered, *If Goldie Roth can't stop worrying, then you must stop being Goldie Roth.*

Goldie frowned. For as long as she could remember she had heard this little voice. It seemed to come from somewhere deep inside her, and until six months ago she had followed its wisdom without question. It was the little voice that had urged her to run away. It had shown her how to navigate the strange, shifting rooms of the Museum of Dunt, and had helped her save Jewel from invasion.

But over the last few months she had got out of the habit of trusting it. All it did was urge her to follow her destiny and become Fifth Keeper, and she could not do that without hurting her parents.

Now, however, she needed its help. She nodded, realising that the little voice was right. Somehow she must stop being Goldie Roth . . .

She was reluctant to leave the front of the bread shop unguarded, but she had little choice – there were things that she must do before nightfall. And besides, everything so far had happened under cover of darkness. She didn't think that Harrow and his men would give their game away by showing themselves in daylight.

'I'll be back,' she whispered, wishing that Toadspit and Bonnie could hear her. 'I'll be back tonight to get you out of there.'

In several places up and down the hill there were enclosed passages that led to the next street. Halfway along one of them, Goldie found a rubbish yard with piles of rags and rotting gazettes, and empty tins of olive oil stacked nearly as high as a house.

She sorted through the rags until she found a pair of old britches and a jacket with one arm. The britches were too big so she tied a string around her waist to hold them up. She unpinned her bird brooch and was about to slip it into her pocket when she paused. She ran her fingers over the outstretched wings and thought about Auntie Praise.

She had never met her aunt – Praise Koch disappeared at the age of sixteen and was never seen again. But Ma sometimes talked sadly about her, saying how brave she had been, and how Goldie was just like her.

Goldie swallowed, and pinned the brooch inside her collar, where it would not be noticed. She rubbed her boots in the oily muck that covered the ground, and smeared some of that same muck on her face. Then she took out Toadspit's knife and sawed off her hair until it was as short as a boy's.

By the time she had finished, she felt different.

Sharper.

Lighter.

Fiercer.

'I am no longer Goldie Roth, who has sick parents and a chain around her heart,' she whispered. 'I'm Goldie No One. No parents. No bad dreams. Just two friends to rescue and take home.'

She buried her own jacket and her smock in the pile of rags. She buried the coil of rope too, so that it would be there when she needed it. Then she set out to learn everything she could about the streets around the bread shop.

This part of Spoke was a winding, confusing place. The cobblestones underfoot reminded Goldie of Jewel, and there were little shrines here and there to Great Wooden or Bald Thoke, or one of the other Seven Gods. But everything else was different. The streets were narrower. The gutters were smellier. The buildings were made of wood instead of bluestone, and there was a brass bell hanging on every corner, with a sign above it, saying, *IN CASE OF FIRE*.

By the time Goldie made her way back to the bread shop, she had a rusty iron lever tucked inside her waistband, a bent wire in her pocket, and a clear picture in her mind of which streets and alleys offered an escape route, and which could easily become a trap. Even more important, she had learned that the bread shop did not have a rear entrance. If she was to break in, she must do it through the front.

The morning was well underway by now, and the shop was packed with customers. Goldie leaned against the wall opposite, watching the comings and goings through half-closed eyes. The lock on the shop door looked new, but she thought she could pick it.

The scent of newly baked bread drifted across the street towards her, and she licked her lips. She could smell sausages too. She pushed herself away from the wall and headed down the hill, wishing she had some money.

Don't go far, whispered the little voice in the back of her mind.

Goldie hesitated, looking over her shoulder at the bread shop and wondering if perhaps she should stay after all. But she was so hungry by now that she felt slightly dizzy. 'I have to find something to eat,' she said, 'or I'll be useless.'

And she kept going down the hill.

As the street flattened out, it grew noisier and more crowded. Goldie stared around, fascinated. Six months after the defeat of the Blessed Guardians, many of Jewel's citizens still lived their lives behind closed doors and didn't dare raise their voices in case someone noticed them. But here in Spoke, people seemed to *want* to be noticed.

A landlady sat on her doorstep, shouting at one of her boarders. 'Where have you been all night? Wipe your feet before you go inside. And where's your rent? Don't smile at me, you rogue. I can't live on a smile, now can I?'

A knife sharpener was setting up his wheel on the footpath. Above his head a woman leaned out an upper-storey window and hung clothes on a washing line strung across the street.

Goldie heard a shout. 'Hey, Sparky! Getting in early for the Festival?'

She spun around. A cook was lounging on the top step of an underground kitchen, taking sly swigs from the bottle in his pocket. And on the other side of the road—

Goldie blinked. On the other side of the road was a man wearing a mask in the shape of a horse's head.

'Yep,' cried the man in the mask. 'You gotta be ready.' His muffled voice sounded as if he was grinning. 'Oooh, feel that fizzing in the air? Quick, ask me how many wives I've got.'

The cook chuckled. 'How many wives you got?'

'Three,' cried Sparky. 'And all of them as fat as pumpkins.'

They both roared with laughter, and the horse man danced away up the street.

Now that Goldie had spotted the first mask, they seemed to be everywhere. Some of them were plain, but most were covered in sequins or fur or the scales of a fish. She passed a stall that sold nothing else, and it was doing a roaring trade.

A little way past the stall she found a plain half-mask lying forgotten on the footpath. She picked it up and tied the strings behind her head, then inspected herself in the nearest window. She looked like a boy. A homeless, anonymous boy.

No one . . .

A snatch of song caught her attention. An old woman selling meat scraps fried in batter was singing about a girl who fell in love with a bear. Her customers joined in the chorus.

'And her children were hairy
And terribly scary
They say . . .'

Despite her hunger and her worries, Goldie felt her heart lift. Spoke reminded her of the Museum of Dunt. It buzzed with life and energy, and she had no idea what was around the next corner. This was what a city *should* be like!

Somewhere nearby, a brass band began to play. As Goldie turned towards the music, she saw a flash of colour, as bright as a parrot, and a short woman wearing a green woollen cloak and a cat mask pushed roughly past her.

The bright green cloak and the cat mask were no stranger than the other sights Goldie had come across that morning. But something made her turn and watch the woman as she elbowed her way up the street.

In the back of her mind, the little voice whispered, *Don't go far!*

Again Goldie hesitated. What if the little voice was right? What if . . .

Her stomach gurgled with hunger. The smell of battered meat scraps and hot pies made her head swim.

She took one last look at the woman in the green cloak and cat mask, and turned away. 'I'll be back by nightfall,' she whispered. 'Nothing will happen before then. I'll get them out tonight.'

THE
BANDMASTER

The brass band wasn't at
all what Goldie had been
expecting. There were
six musicians plus a bandmaster,
and she had seldom seen a more
mismatched bunch of people. They
were tall and short, men and women,
hairy and clean-shaven. They wore
ill-fitting striped suits and
shuffled around a fountain
in the middle of a stone-
flagged plaza. Their music
rose and fell in waves, sometimes

The Bandmaster

stopping right in the middle of a tune, then starting up again with all the instruments out of time.

The bandmaster was a small man with a freckled scalp who waved his baton in the air and bellowed to the watching crowd. Goldie could just hear his voice above the music. It was accompanied by an oddly familiar clanking sound.

'If you please, Herroen and Frowen! A crust of bread for our breakfast, or a sausage. Feed the hungry and the Seven Gods will ignore you for a whole year!'

Goldie flicked her fingers. The Seven Gods were known for their unpredictable tempers. Attracting their attention – even hearing someone mention their names – could be a dangerous business. Flicking your fingers was a polite way of saying, '*Please* don't bother yourself with me, Great Wooden. Go and help someone else.'

A woman in the watching crowd held up a cooked chicken. 'Hoy!' she shouted, and she threw the chicken towards the band.

Immediately the musicians stopped playing and surged forward in a mass. But they were slow and clumsy, and a ragged girl darted out of the crowd and grabbed the chicken from under the hairy trumpeter's nose.

The band members groaned. The crowd parted. And now at last Goldie could see what was causing that horrible clanking sound. The musicians wore shackles around their ankles, and a heavy chain that linked them together and scraped against the cobblestones as they walked.

Goldie shivered, remembering the punishment chains that still haunted her dreams.

There was another shout from the crowd. Quite a few people were throwing food now. Sausages, wheels of cheese, a *whole stuffed goose* tumbled through the air.

The musicians lurched this way and that, grabbing frantically. The one-eyed bombardon player managed to catch a string of sausages. The tall trombonist reached over everyone's head to snatch up a cheese. But the stuffed goose, and a great deal more, was lost to the darting boys and girls.

Goldie's mouth watered. Almost before she knew what she was doing, she found herself elbowing her way into the pack of children. They glanced sideways at her, but said nothing. Their mouths were wet with grease. They sucked their fingers and grinned at each other.

'A goose,' Goldie whispered. 'I could eat a whole goose.'

Someone in the crowd threw a pie, but it was too far away to bother with. Next came a flurry of little fried cakes, then some oranges. The children got most of them.

Goldie inched forward, waiting for the right moment. And then she saw it. A leg of roast mutton sailed through the air towards the bandmaster. He gathered up his chain, so that he would have room to leap . . .

Quick as a gull, Goldie dived in front of him and snatched the mutton from his grasping hands. 'Noooo!' he wailed, as she darted away with her prize.

The meat was still hot, and dripping with rosemary and olive oil. It smelled better than anything Goldie had ever smelled in her life. Carefully she carried it up onto the fountain, hacked off a slice with Toadspit's knife and stuffed it into her mouth, beneath the mask. She closed her eyes, to savour it better . . .

When she opened them again, the grey-spotted cat from the ship was standing in front of her. Its ribs stuck out like the hoops of a barrel. Its wild eyes were fixed on the mutton.

'Do you want some?' said Goldie. She cut another slice and held it out. The cat's nose twitched, but it did not move.

Goldie shrugged, too hungry to be patient. 'I'll eat it if you don't want it.'

The wild eyes glared at her. There was nothing soft in their depths, nothing but distrust and hunger, but Goldie found herself suddenly thinking of the museum, and of Broo, the brizzlehound. She bit her lip, and placed the piece of mutton beside her foot. There was a flash of movement, too quick to follow, and both cat and mutton were gone.

She cut another slice for herself. Mutton grease ran down her chin and she wiped it off, and licked her fingers. She heard a groan. The music had stopped and the bandmaster was staring up at her, his face sagging with misery.

The mutton turned to ashes in Goldie's mouth. She flushed and tried to look away, but the man's unhappy gaze held her. She could hear Olga Ciavolga's voice in her ear, as clearly as if the old woman sat beside her.

'To move quietly, to be quick of hand and eye, that is a gift. If you use it to hurt other people, even in a small way, you betray yourself and everyone around you.'

Like all the keepers of the Museum of Dunt, Olga Ciavolga was a thief. But she had very strict rules about when it was all right to steal and when it was not. And this was not.

With a sigh, Goldie climbed down from the fountain and pushed her way through the crowd, which was thinner now. Most of the food had been thrown and people were wandering away. The children had raced off, chucking oranges at each other.

'We'll be here again tomorrow, Herroen and Frowen,' said the bandmaster wearily. 'Don't forget. Feed the hungry, the Seven Gods will ignore you, blah blah blah.' He sounded as if he didn't expect anyone to feed him ever again.

The musicians tucked their instruments under their arms and began to shuffle across the plaza. Goldie hurried after them. 'Um, Herro—' she said.

The bandmaster's face sagged even further. 'Come to gloat, have you, lad? Come to wave my rightful breakfast under my nose—'

Goldie held the mutton out to him. He broke off, blinking. 'You're right, Herro, it's yours,' she muttered, trying to sound like a boy.

The bandmaster stared at her as if he thought it might be a trick. She thrust the mutton into his hands and turned away, before she could change her mind.

'Wait,' mumbled the bandmaster.

Goldie looked back at him. He had already bitten a mouthful of meat straight off the leg and was chewing desperately, as if he hadn't eaten for days. The bombardon player was patting him on the back and trying to sneak pieces of mutton. He batted her hands away and beckoned to Goldie.

'Come here, come here, lad. Don't be afraid.'

As Goldie retraced her steps, the musicians stared at her. 'Am I right in thinking you have a knife?' said the bandmaster, wiping his mouth on his striped sleeve.

Goldie nodded.

The bandmaster made a stiff little bow. 'Would you be so good as to cut a slice for each of my companions here? And – ah – another slice for yourself?'

Goldie didn't wait to be asked twice. While the bandmaster held the mutton steady, she whipped out her knife and cut off several big chunks.

'Ah— Perhaps a little smaller,' said the bandmaster hastily. 'My companions have eaten this morning, after all, and I have not.'

'Sorry,' said Goldie, and she cut the chunks into pieces.

'Yes, yes, that's better,' said the bandmaster, watching the meat hungrily. 'And some for you – good, good. And now I believe it is my turn again. Yes, definitely my turn.'

With his mouth full, he said, 'Would you care to walk with us? We must not be late, but I am curious—' He broke off and licked his lips. 'Mm, that is truly the sweetest mutton I have tasted for years. Hardly mutton at all. I suspect it was lamb only yesterday, prancing in the fields beside its doting mother. Are you too busy eating, or could you cut me another slice?'

'Where are you going, Herro?' said Goldie, hacking at the meat as they walked. 'Why are you – um—' She pointed to the chains.

The bandmaster peered at her. 'You're not from around here? Well, that would explain your generosity. I have never heard of one of the street snotties giving back a prize before. And *such* a prize!'

'I'm from Jewel,' said Goldie.

'Aha, I thought so. And *I* am from the Spoke Penitentiary.' He bowed again, as if he had just announced that he was the governor of the city. 'As are all my friends here.'

'You're *prisoners*?' said Goldie.

'Dear me, no. We're guests! If we were prisoners they would have to feed us all year round. But because we are merely guests, they can turf us out during the Festival to find our own sustenance.'

He wiped his hand on his britches, and pulled out a battered pocket watch. 'Of course we have to be back in our cells at a certain time, or they will forget the politeness that is due to guests.' He waggled the leg of mutton at Goldie. 'Cut me another slice, my boy. And help yourself. I can see you're not the greedy sort.'

Goldie cut another two slices. 'What's the Festival?'

'Why, the Festival of Lies,' said the bandmaster. 'Starts officially the day after tomorrow. Everyone likes to build up to it, which is why we are here, two days early, and not tucked up snug in our cells with a bowl of hot porridge in front of us. Although—' he chewed thoughtfully, 'I do believe I would sacrifice a dozen bowls of porridge for this glorious feast.'

'Why is it called the Festival of Lies?'

'Because that's what it is. For three days, the entire city turns upside down and back to front. No one tells the truth – unless they're touching an animal, of course.'

Goldie had a dozen more questions on the tip of her tongue, but the bandmaster was still talking. 'It's a good time for us, the Festival. Did you hear me, back by the fountain?' He raised his baton dramatically. 'Feed the hungry, and the Seven Gods will ignore you for a whole year!'

Goldie flicked her fingers.

The bandmaster grinned. 'It works, too, and everyone in Spoke knows it.' He lowered his voice. 'Of course, they *could* throw half-chewed crusts and boiled tripe and it would work just as well. But we've spread the word that the *better* they feed us, the more likely the Gods are to ignore them.'

They had reached the other side of the plaza by now, and the musicians began to hurry, as fast as their chains would let them, through the winding streets. Goldie trotted beside them, watching for landmarks so she could find her way back again. An idea was growing inside her.

'Why were you imprisoned, Herro?' she said. 'If you don't mind me asking.'

'Don't mind at all, lad,' said the bandmaster. 'And you know why? Because I'm innocent.' He waved the leg of mutton at the musicians who rattled along behind him. 'We're all innocent. Young Dodger there, with the trumpet, is innocent of robbery with violence. Sweetapple is innocent of poisoning her husband, may Great Wooden rot his soul.' He flicked his fingers. So did Goldie. 'And Old Snot – that's him dribbling over the bass drum – is innocent of running a gang of pickpockets.'

Old Snot grinned toothlessly at Goldie. Sweetapple, who was the tall trombonist with the limp, waved.

'What are you – er – innocent of?' said Goldie to the bandmaster.

'Forgery.' He struck a serious pose with his hand on his heart. 'I did not do it, Your Honour. I have no idea how those fake coins came to be in my cellar. I am *not* a criminal.'

He winked at Goldie, and she laughed. 'If I wanted to find out about someone who *is* a criminal,' she said, 'who would I ask?'

The bandmaster puffed out his chest. 'I have lived in Spoke all my life. No one has his finger on the city's pulse the way I do. What's his name, this criminal of yours?'

'Harrow.'

Goldie wasn't expecting what happened next. The bandmaster seemed to trip over something. His baton flew out of his hand and clattered onto the cobblestones. The leg of mutton tumbled into the gutter.

'Halt!' he cried. With a great clanking of chains, Sweetapple and the rest of the band shuffled to a stop behind him. The bandmaster picked up the baton and the meat, and brushed the dirt off them. 'No harm done,' he said.

He turned back to Goldie. 'Now, what were we talking about, lad?'

'Um— Harrow,' said Goldie.

The bandmaster screwed up his face, as if he was thinking. 'Noooo, can't say I've ever heard the name. Is he a local man?'

'I don't know.'

'There you are then. He's probably from Lawe. A most disreputable city, Lawe. All the worst criminals come from there.'

He took out his pocket watch again. 'Oops, we're late. Pick up those chains,' he roared at the band. 'Double time! Hup two three four, hup two three four!'

As they jogged off, he glanced over his shoulder at Goldie. '*So* pleased to meet an honest lad,' he cried. Sweetapple waved again, and Dodger winked. Then, with a great deal of noise, they were gone.

Goldie stood unmoving in the middle of the street. Despite the roast mutton, a hollow feeling had opened up inside her. As a trained liar, she could tell when someone else was lying.

The bandmaster *did* know Harrow. And the name struck fear into his heart.

THE MUSEUM OF DUNT

'Over the last few days,' said Sinew, drumming his fingers on the kitchen table, 'I have tracked a hundred different rumours. I've learned that the citizens of Lawe are plotting against their government, that Old Lady Skint has a new slave ship, and that the mercenary army that was terrorising the Southern Archipelago has left for unknown shores. But about the children I've discovered nothing.'

Sinew

In the basket by the stove, little dog Broo whimpered in his sleep.

'Whoever has taken them,' said Sinew, 'has covered their tracks too well. I need to go and search for them myself.'

The sharp-eyed old woman who sat opposite him shook her head. Despite the warmth of the stove, she wore a blanket over her shoulders, as well as two knitted jerkins and four or five skirts. Her feet were thrust into militia boots. 'We cannot spare you, Sinew.'

'But we can't simply leave them—'

Sinew's protest was cut off by the third person at the table, an old man with a broad brown face, and brass buttons down the front of his jacket. 'Olga Ciavolga's right,' he said. 'We need you here, lad. The rooms are gettin' restless again.'

The Museum of Dunt was never entirely quiet – there was so much wildness contained within its walls that its rooms regularly shuffled back and forth like a giant pack of cards.

But ever since the children had gone missing, that shuffling had grown worse. Even now, in the middle of the night, the gallery known as Vermin whispered and twitched, and the ancient dangers of war, famine and plague, locked away deep inside the museum, woke from their dreams and looked around with bright, vicious eyes.

'This place don't like it when its friends are in trouble,' said Herro Dan.

'All the more reason,' said Sinew, 'for me to go and look for the children! The sooner they're back here, the better for everyone.'

Olga Ciavolga nodded. 'That is true. But think on this, Sinew. Right now there are *three* children in peril. If you go, and Dan and I lose control of the museum, every child in the city will suffer a terrible fate. And so will the adults.'

Sinew leaned back in his chair and blew out a frustrated breath. 'You're right, of course. It's just— We *know* these three! They are our friends. And I can't help worrying about them.'

Olga Ciavolga raised an eyebrow. 'Do you think you are the only one who is worried?'

'No, of course not. But what have we done, apart from chasing useless rumours? Nothing! They must think we've deserted them—'

'What about Morg?' interrupted Herro Dan. 'She's a good finder, our Morg. We could send *her* to look for 'em.'

There was a whirr of wings from the rafters overhead, and an enormous black shape swooped down and landed on the old man's shoulder. 'Mo-o-o-o-org,' croaked the slaughterbird.

71

'Yes, I'm talkin' about you,' said Herro Dan. He smiled and scratched the bird's chest fondly, then his face grew serious again. 'Do you reckon you can find 'em for us? I dunno where they might be.'

Sinew leaned forward. 'Look out to sea, Morg. Try and find the ship that took them. And if you don't have any luck there, try the cities.'

'Look for thefts,' said Olga Ciavolga, 'big and small. Look for the shadow that a theft leaves on the air.'

'And if you find the children—' said Herro Dan.

'*When* you find them,' corrected Sinew.

The old man nodded. 'When you find 'em, do your best to help 'em. And bring 'em back safely.'

'Ba-a-a-a-ack,' croaked Morg, shifting from foot to foot to make sure that the old man scratched the right spot.

'All right then.' Herro Dan stood up and opened the kitchen door. 'No point hangin' around. Off you go.'

The bird on his shoulder bobbed her head several times. Then, with a great flurry of feathers, she launched herself out into the corridor.

As the sound of her wings faded, Sinew heaved a sigh. 'That's something, I suppose. But I wish—' He picked up his harp, and half a dozen anxious notes trickled out into the kitchen. 'I wish we knew where

72

the children were! I wish we knew what was happening to them!'

'Museum'll tell us soon enough,' said Herro Dan. 'If the rooms settle down, then the children are safe, and on their way home. But if things keep gettin' worse—'

He stopped. All three keepers looked grimly at each other. In the basket by the stove, Broo began to whimper again and would not be comforted.

In the street outside the bread shop, everything was quiet. Goldie crouched in the darkness of the doorway, her mask firmly in place.

She had not used a picklock for six months, but her fingers had not forgotten their skill. She slid the bent wire into the keyhole above the blade of her knife, and began to push the pins up, one by one. As each pin slid out of the way, she heard a faint click.

Several streets away, a man was singing loudly and drunkenly about a lost child. Goldie tried not to listen. *Concentrate,* she told herself.

The last pin clicked into place. Quickly she glanced up and down the street, then pushed the door. It opened a crack and stopped. The door was barred from inside.

Goldie took the iron lever from her waistband and eased it through the gap until she could feel the bar. She braced herself and pushed the lever upwards. The bar rose smoothly—

Stop! hissed the little voice in the back of her mind.

Goldie stopped. She stepped away from the door for the space of five breaths, and let the night air tuck around her like a blanket. Then she gripped the lever in cold hands, and started again.

This time she pushed the bar up so carefully that anyone watching would hardly have seen it move. When she came to the place where she had stopped before, she paused. She pressed her ear to the gap. She shifted the lever a hair's width – and heard the faint scrape of a wire.

Carefully she backed the lever off and slid her makeshift picklock through the gap. There was the wire. Now, if she could just hook it in place – *exactly* in place – so the wire would not move while she lifted the bar – gently now, *gently*—

She had it. The bar rose and slid to one side. The wire strained to move, but she would not let it. With her heart in her throat she eased the door open just far enough, and squeezed through into the gloom of the bread shop.

Something brushed against her leg. She gasped and

74

nearly let go of the wire. The grey-spotted cat glared up at her, then dashed behind the counter.

'Are you following me?' whispered Goldie. 'What do you want?'

There was no answer, of course. She shrugged, hoping the cat would not make a nuisance of itself, and turned to inspect the door.

It was as she had thought. There was a row of alarum bells hanging above the lintel. She reached up and disconnected them. Then she unhooked the picklock, leaned against the door with her eyes closed, and let her body and her mind settle into the stillness of the Third Method of Concealment.

Imitation of Nothingness was one of the most important things she had learned in her training as a thief. It didn't make her invisible, but it *did* make her unimportant. *So* unimportant that even the light passed over her without stopping. As long as she moved slowly, there wasn't one person in ten thousand who could see her.

I am dust in the moonlight. I am a forgotten dream. I am nothing . . .

Her mind began to drift outwards, until she could sense every nearby scrap of life, big and small, awake and asleep. There was the cat, crouched behind the counter, its pulse beating with a feral hunger. There were rats and cowbeetles in the walls, and cockroaches going about their secret business. And somewhere in the rooms at the back of the shop, four human hearts – two adults and two children – tolled out the slow rhythms of midnight.

Goldie listened to those rhythms carefully. The children must be Bonnie and Toadspit. But who were the adults? Was Harrow here? She remembered how the bandmaster had shrunk in fear at the name, and her throat clenched. But at the same time she felt a bubble of anger. The people of Jewel used to shrink like that, whenever the Blessed Guardians passed by. Goldie had hated it then, and she hated it now.

I bet Harrow likes making people afraid, she thought. *I bet he likes squashing people. Well, he's not going to squash me!*

She opened her eyes. The bread shop dozed around her, heavy with the smell of yeast. There were flagstones under her feet and, at the back of the shop, a small square doorway. Like a shadow, Goldie drifted towards it. The cat slipped out from behind the counter and prowled after her.

The first room she came to held an enormous brick oven. There were no windows, and it was so dark that she had to feel her way around the walls, avoiding the stacks of empty tins.

The next room was a kitchen and scullery. The heartbeats were closer now. Goldie crept towards them – then stopped, uncertain.

'Why is everyone sleeping so peacefully?' she whispered to the cat. 'Shouldn't someone be keeping watch over the prisoners? Shouldn't Toadspit be trying to escape? Maybe he's still unconscious!'

The cat sneered at her, as if it knew something that she didn't.

And suddenly it struck Goldie that the bread shop didn't feel at all like a place with stolen children in it. Instead it felt . . . *relieved*, as if something dangerous had happened, but now it was over and done with, and the shop's inhabitants could relax again.

She slid into the first bedroom, trying to ignore the sinking feeling in her stomach. *I am nothing. I am the memory of a cooling oven . . .*

On one side of the iron-framed bed, a woman was snoring, her mouth open and a frayed bedcap covering her hair. Next to her, the bread-shop man, his eyebrows dusted with flour, mumbled in his dreams.

Goldie left them sleeping, and stole into the next room, where the two children lay in bunks. She peered hopefully at them—

But they were strangers.

The sinking feeling grew worse. She tried to push it

away; Bonnie and Toadspit must be here somewhere; they *must* be! Perhaps they were imprisoned behind a very thick door, and that was why she couldn't feel them . . .

The last three rooms were storerooms. The first and the second had no windows, and were not locked. They were both empty. Goldie stood in the darkness, listening to her own breathing. One room to go.

She hardly dared approach it. She saw the heavy door with the bolt on the outside, and her hopes rose and fell in sickening swoops.

She slid the bolt back.

She eased the door open.

Unlike the others, the third storeroom had a tiny window. But the gaslight that filtered in from outside showed nothing but bare walls, and a number of hessian bags strewn willy nilly across the floor, as if someone had thrown them down in a temper.

Goldie slumped back against the door. She felt like crying. Somewhere outside the window a dog barked, but she hardly heard it. She could no longer ignore the awful truth. Bonnie and Toadspit were not here. They must have been moved while she was walking around the city.

'Idiot!' she whispered fiercely, wishing that she had listened more carefully to the little voice. 'You've lost them!'

The grey-spotted cat slunk past her into the room. 'What am I supposed to do now, cat?' whispered Goldie, wishing that Broo was here, instead of this unfriendly creature.

The cat ignored her. It stared at the hessian sacks, its tail twitching from side to side. In the far corner of the room, something scratched at the floor. The cat's head swivelled towards it.

The scratching sound came again. The cat's bony hindquarters began to tremble. It inched across the floor on silent paws. It sprang. There was a squeak of terror, then nothing.

Goldie swallowed, trying not to think about what might have happened to her friends. The cat sidled past her, a small, limp corpse dangling from its jaws.

'He wants *what*?' said the Protector.

The captain of militia cleared his throat. 'He wants to help, Your Grace. Sorry to bother you at this time of night, but one of the guards told him about the children going missing, and he reckons he might be able to find them. I thought you'd want to know as soon as possible.'

The Protector pushed her hair out of her eyes. She should have been in bed hours ago, but she could not sleep for worry about the missing children. And now there was this ridiculous offer from the Fugleman. 'He's in a prison cell!' she snapped. 'How could he possibly find *anything*? Except perhaps for bedbugs.'

'He says he's got contacts, Your Grace. People he's worked with all over the peninsula, and in the Southern Archipelago too. They're not a nice bunch – he admits he's been a bad boy. But that's all the better, Your Grace. If it's criminals or slavers who've taken the children, then who better to find them than other criminals and slavers?'

The Protector felt the old anger welling up inside her. 'Tell the Fugleman – the *ex*-Fugleman – that we do not need—'

She forced herself to stop. Perhaps she should not be so hasty. After all, Sinew's enquiries had come to nothing, and so had hers . . .

'Why is he offering this?' she said. 'What does he want? Money? Or is he trying to worm his way back into favour?'

'He claims to be genuinely remorseful, Your Grace.'

The Protector laughed grimly. 'I am sure he does. But what's his *real* reason?'

'Maybe— Maybe he's hoping for a lighter sentence.'

'Mm. I suppose that could be it.'

'If he's genuine, Your Grace, there's no harm done. And his villainous friends might just be able to help.'

'And if it's a trick?'

'Then we need to expose it as soon as possible.'

The Protector pushed her chair back. 'What does he need?'

'He wants to send out lots of semaphore messages, that's all. He says he can do it from the House of Repentance if you'll let him into the office and give him a runner.'

'I still don't like it.'

'He'll be under close guard, Your Grace. And we'll make sure that the messages are read before they are sent. We won't give him a chance to get up to any of his nonsense.'

'I suppose—' The Protector sighed. She was feeling old. 'If there's a chance it will help find the children, then I must allow it.'

'You won't regret it, Your Grace,' said the captain.

'I do hope not,' said the Protector. 'I really do hope not.'

THE WHITE-HAIRED BOY

Goldie spent the rest of that miserable night curled up next to the chimney of an underground kitchen. She dozed fitfully, and when the sounds of clattering saucepans echoed up from below, just before dawn, she crawled to her feet, pulled her torn jacket close and went back to the bread

Mouse

shop. The air was colder than ever and the hunger was as sharp as flint in her stomach.

She could see movement in the back of the shop, but the doors weren't yet open, and the only people around were other ragged children scouring the cobblestones for crusts.

Goldie joined them and found enough to take the worst edge off her hunger. She also found the wheel marks from the horse and cart and followed them for two blocks before they were lost under a hundred other such marks.

In the back of her mind, the little voice whispered, *You're missing something*.

Goldie returned to the shop and watched it for most of the morning, mingling with the passersby. There was no sign of the cat, and nothing happened that would lead her to her friends.

But in the back of her mind the little voice whispered again, *Missing something . . .*

She did her best to work out what she might have missed in her midnight search. But there was nothing, she was sure of it. Not unless you counted stacks of bread tins and empty hessian bags.

Just before midday, she gave up her vigil, hid the iron lever in the pile of rays next to the rope, and set out to search the rest of the city. The streets were crowded, and she wished desperately that Toadspit was with her, and that they were looking for Bonnie together. She wished, too, that she could talk to Olga Ciavolga, or Herro Dan, or Sinew. She felt horribly lonely and did not know what she could do in the afternoon that was any better than what she had done in the morning.

In the cellars of her mind, the little voice whispered, *Missing something . . . missing something . . .*

The sun was already low in the winter sky when she found herself in another plaza, a smaller one than yesterday's. There were shops all around the edges, with canvas awnings folded back, and dark interiors. In front of the shops, cinnamon, nutmeg, peppercorns and powdered ginger spilled from their sacks. There were stone jars of honey, too, and coffee and cocoa beans.

In the middle of the plaza, a crowd had gathered. Goldie wriggled through it, hoping for something to eat. Instead she found a small boy with white hair and bare feet standing next to a rickety-looking pram. The pram had a board nailed across the top of it and was filled to the brim with scraps of paper.

A man at the front of the crowd held up a coin. 'Here, lad,' he said. 'Tell *my* fortune.'

The boy, who looked to be about six or seven years old, was very thin, and his feet were blue with the cold. But there was something cheerful about him that immediately raised Goldie's battered spirits. He took the coin, slipped it into his pocket and whistled softly.

There was a rustling sound, and the pram rocked on its springs. A moment later, a white mouse with a scrap of paper between its teeth scrambled up onto the board. It was quickly followed by another mouse, and another, and another. Before long there were twelve of them lined up, each with its bit of paper. They were all pure white with little pink eyes and pink ears, and they gazed up at the boy as if they were waiting for instructions.

He whistled again, and they dropped their bits of paper onto the board.

'Is that it?' said the man, taking a step forward.

The boy held up his hand, as if to say, 'Wait.' He tipped his head to one side and stared at the bits of paper. From where Goldie stood, they looked as if they had been torn out of books and gazettes. Some of them had only one word on them, others had a whole sentence. Two of them had no words at all, only pictures, though Goldie couldn't see what they were.

The boy moved the scraps of paper around, tossing some of them back into the pram. When he was satisfied, he nodded.

'Well,' said the man, winking at his friends, 'let's see what's in store for me.'

He stabbed his finger at the bits of paper one by one, and read them out loud. '*Cotton socklets* – ah, that'll be something to do with my business.' He nodded approvingly. 'It's a good start, lad. I don't make socklets exactly, but you've got the cotton bit right. Now, what comes next? *Long hand.* What's that got to do with anything? And the next one, *sick one day*. Is this supposed to make sense?'

The white-haired boy shrugged.

The man stared at the bits of paper, puzzled. Then his face cleared, and he turned to one of his companions, who had a snub nose and an arm in splints. 'Hang on, young Spider, I think it's talking about you! Long hand, that's close enough to arm, isn't it?' He beamed at the crowd. 'Spider's my accountant. Broke his arm yesterday, poor sod. Those mice are smart little beggars, aren't they?'

The crowd peered at the young man, who flushed, as if he was too shy to enjoy such attention.

His boss poked at the next bit of paper. 'Ooh, now we're getting interesting. *Do not betray me, oh my darling*. Sounds like something out of a bad romance. And this next one. *Five hundred thousand thalers.*'

He laughed, but it seemed to Goldie that he was not quite as amused as he had been. Spider's face had lost some of its colour.

The man turned to the white-haired boy. 'Is this a true fortune?'

The boy nodded.

'Festival doesn't start till tomorrow, lad. You can't get away with lies today. You sure it's true?'

The boy nodded again.

The man bent over the remaining scraps of paper. Goldie saw his face darken. He swore under his breath. Then, with one quick movement, he spun around and grabbed Spider's good arm.

The accountant flinched and tried to pull away, but the man held him tightly. 'Going on a little trip, Spider?' he growled.

'Y-you know I am, Herro Metz,' stammered Spider. 'Y-you gave me permission to visit my mother, who lives down the coast. Just until my arm is healed.'

'Ah, yes, the arm,' said Herro Metz. 'Where exactly is it broken?'

'Th-there, Herro.' Spider pointed to a spot below his elbow. 'A simple break, nothing too serious. I'll be back at work before you know it.'

Herro Metz peered at him closely. Then, to Goldie's surprise, he smiled. 'Of course you will,' he said. 'I never doubted it.' And he let go of the accountant's arm.

The crowd sighed. The colour began to creep back into Spider's cheeks. But before he could speak, Herro

Metz's hand lashed out again and grabbed the broken arm – just below the elbow.

Spider was so shocked that it took him a second or two to respond. Then he mumbled, 'Ouch.'

It was not even slightly convincing. An angry murmur ran through the crowd. Herro Metz leaned over the young man. 'You and I, Spider,' he growled, 'need to have a little chat about money. *Now!*'

As the two of them disappeared into the crowd, Goldie heard Spider's frightened voice. 'I— I was going to pay it back, Herro, really I was. It was just a – a loan.'

The crowd stared after them. One or two people took out coins, as if they wanted *their* fortunes told. But then they thought better of it, and put their money away. Before long they had all wandered off.

Goldie peered at the remaining scraps of paper. The first had a picture of a ship on it. The second said *the greatest escape of*.

'How did they know?' she asked the white-haired boy. 'All that stuff about the accountant. How did the mice know which bits of paper to pull out?'

The boy smiled shyly, but didn't answer. He whisked the pieces of paper back into the pram, then held out his hand to the mice. They scurried up to perch on his shoulders and head, and began to clean themselves, licking their tiny paws and brushing up their whiskers and ears. Every now and then one of them would break off to clean the boy's ears instead, or to nibble the ragged ends of his hair.

Suddenly, one of them squeaked a warning. A dozen heads shot up. A dozen furry backs bristled.

Goldie turned around. Stalking across the cobblestones, its eyes fixed on the mice, was the grey-spotted cat.

'Go away!' said Goldie, and she stamped her foot.

The cat took no notice of her. All of its attention was on the mice. Its tail thrashed from side to side. Its teeth chattered. It pressed its scrawny haunches to the ground . . .

Then it sprang.

GREAT DANGER

The boy threw up his arms to protect his mice. At the same time, the mice leaped for the safety of the pram.

Some of them were quicker than others. The three on the boy's head waited until the very last minute, as if they couldn't bear to desert him. By the time they jumped, the cat was already changing direction. It landed squarely on the board across the pram and

The Cat

spread its claws, ready to scoop up the last three mice as they arrived.

But somehow they too managed to change direction. With their feet flailing and their little eyes bulging with fright, they missed the pram altogether and fell onto the cobblestones.

The cat sprang after them, its eyes blazing.

'No!' cried Goldie. And she grabbed Toadspit's still-folded knife from her pocket and threw it with all her strength.

It hit the cat on the side of the head and stunned it momentarily. The mice raced across the cobble-stones and dived into a drain. Before the cat could gather its wits and follow them, the boy threw himself upon it.

'Be careful!' cried Goldie, remembering what had happened to Harrow's fighting dog.

The boy quickly bent his head and crooned something, and although the cat hissed and yowled it kept its claws sheathed.

Goldie picked up the knife and put it back in her pocket. The boy raised his eyebrows at her, as if he was asking a question, then looked towards the drain.

'You want me to get the mice?' said Goldie, who was still worried about the cat and what it might do.

The boy nodded. The cat twisted in his arms, but he

held it against his chest and began to whistle to it, the way he had whistled to the mice.

Goldie crouched in front of the drain. At first she couldn't see anything, but then her eyes adjusted to the darkness and she could just make out three bundles of trembling white fur.

She reached out her hand. 'Here, mousie,' she whispered. Three pairs of pink eyes blinked nervously at her. 'I'm sorry about the cat,' she said. 'I should've known it'd turn up again. It's been following me.'

She kept her voice low and her hand very still and, before long, one of the mice began to groom itself. The others joined in, slicking their fur and cleaning their paws and whiskers. Gradually their trembling stopped.

Goldie glanced over her shoulder. The boy's eyes were half-closed and he was blinking sleepily down at the cat. To Goldie's astonishment, the cat was blinking back at him and purring in a crackly, unpractised voice. All of its fierce, sharp angles had softened, and now she could see the elegance that lay beneath.

'I think your boy has tamed the cat,' she whispered to the mice. 'You can come out now.'

The mice gave their paws a final lick, and tidied their whiskers. Then, one by one, they trooped towards her hand, inspected it carefully, and climbed on board.

Goldie had no idea what the cat might do when it

saw the mice again, so she hid them against her jacket. They wriggled in her hand, full of life and warmth, and she wished she could keep them there forever.

But the boy was already lowering the cat to the ground and holding his own hand out for his pets. Reluctantly, Goldie gave them back. When they smelled their enemy on the boy's skin they squeaked in protest.

The cat's ears swivelled. It crouched down, its eyes fixed on the boy's hand, its tail lashing.

It was then that the white-haired boy did something that amazed Goldie. With the palm of his hand flat, and the three mice sitting there, unprotected, he squatted next to the cat.

'I don't think—' she began.

But the boy wasn't listening to her. He was explaining to the cat and the mice that they must be friends. At least, that's what it sounded like to Goldie, although the noise he made was nothing more than a humming croon.

The cat's ears flicked back and forth as if it was thinking unfamiliar thoughts. Slowly, its fierceness drained away. It took a step forward. For a moment the mice looked as if they were trying to be brave, but then their nerve broke and they ran up the boy's arm and dived inside his jacket.

The boy crooned a bit more. The cat sat down so close to his hand that its whiskers touched his fingertips. Its spotted limbs were as still as a statue of Great Wooden. Its eyes blinked sleepily.

One by one, the mice poked their heads out from inside the boy's jacket. One by one they crept back down his arm to the palm of his hand. They craned forward until they were almost touching the cat's whiskers. Their noses crinkled. They shook their little heads and sneezed.

Then they sat down and began to clean themselves, as if they were in the safest place in the world.

Goldie let out her breath with a loud *huff*. 'How did you *do* that?'

The boy stood up, grinning, and put the mice back in the pram. The cat lounged amiably against his feet, as if it had never in its life thought of harming another creature.

Very quickly and lightly, the boy put his hand on Goldie's arm, then took it away again.

'What?' said Goldie.

The boy pointed at the pram.

'You want me to wheel the pram? No. You want to *give* me the pram? No, I didn't think so. Oh, you want to tell my fortune.'

The boy nodded. Goldie swallowed, thinking of Toadspit and Bonnie. A fortune might tell her where to find them. Or at least give her some sort of clue. 'I haven't got any money,' she said.

The boy shrugged and whistled.

This time, when the mice scrambled up onto the board with their scraps of paper, Goldie knew what to expect. She waited impatiently while the boy shifted the scraps around, making a picture of shapes and colours that pleased him.

By the time he had finished, there were only four bits of paper left. The first was a picture of a very high mountain. The second one simply said *danger*. The third said *friendship is*. The fourth was two entire sentences that looked as if they had been torn from a book. *You are still here, Herro. Does this mean you will help me?*

Goldie's heart sank. It didn't seem to have anything to do with Bonnie and Toadspit, except perhaps for the bit about danger. But why was there a picture of a mountain?

'Does it mean mountains are dangerous?' she said. 'But we're not near any. So maybe it's not meant to be a *real* mountain. Just— Just something rocky. No, something big. Look at it, it's huge. So maybe it means, um, *huge* danger. No, *great* danger, that's it.'

A shiver ran down her spine. *Harrow* . . .

The boy touched her arm again, as light as a moth.

'Sorry,' said Goldie, and she read the second half of her fortune out loud. The boy's eyes widened. He tapped his chest, then pointed to the mice and the cat.

'Friendship,' said Goldie. 'And someone to help me. Do you think it means you?'

The boy pointed to the mice and the cat again.

'You think it means *all* of you?'

The boy beamed at her. Then he grabbed the handle of the pram and set off across the plaza with the cat close at his heels. Goldie didn't move.

When he realised that she wasn't following him, the boy turned and beckoned. Goldie was tempted to go with him. But she was heading into great danger, and did not want anyone else to be harmed because of it. So she waved instead and called out, 'Thanks for the fortune.'

The boy beckoned again. In the back of Goldie's mind, the little voice whispered, *Go with him.* She ignored it and turned away.

She had not gone far when she felt something bump against her legs. The cat gazed up at her. 'M-rrow?'

She tried to keep walking, but with every step it wound itself between her ankles. 'Watch out,' she said.

'Frrr-own,' said the cat, almost as if it was talking to her. And it sat down directly in front of her.

Goldie stepped around it. It shifted so quickly that she barely saw it move, and sat down again.

She glared at it. 'What do you *want*?'

'Prrrowl,' demanded the cat, and it raised its ragged

tail high in the air and began to stalk back the way it had come, stopping occasionally to look over its shoulder. On the other side of the plaza, the boy watched them both.

Go with them, whispered the little voice.

'No,' said Goldie. 'I don't want to.'

It was a lie and she knew it. The sun had almost disappeared behind the buildings that surrounded the Spice Market, and a cold wind was blowing up from the harbour. Soon it would be dark. If she walked away now, she realised, she would have to spend another night alone. And perhaps another one after that.

She didn't think she could bear it.

The cat turned towards her. 'All right,' said Goldie quickly. 'I'll come.'

'Nnnn-ow?' said the cat.

'Yes. Now.'

A MESSAGE
FROM TOADSPIT

The Brizzlehound

The white-haired boy lived in a sewer. It was very old, and big enough to walk through, and it obviously hadn't been used for many years. But it was still a sewer, and its brick sides were crusted with slime.

Goldie followed the boy into the darkness. The pram wheels rattled and clanked over the rough ground, and she could hear water dripping somewhere. Cockroaches scuttled past her feet. The cat stalked behind her like a jailer.

'Where are we going?' she whispered, knowing that there would be no answer.

She thought she could probably trust the white-haired boy, but she had no idea who else might be living down here. And so, when she saw a faint yellow glow ahead, she stopped. Her foot kicked against a stone. It was only the slightest of sounds, but the glow snuffed out immediately.

The air moved, as if someone was creeping down the tunnel towards her. Goldie's skin crawled.

'Oo's this, Mousie?' whispered a hoarse voice. 'Whatchoo doin', bringin' someone down 'ere?'

It sounded like a boy. Goldie roughened her own voice. 'I'm – ah – lookin' for a place to sleep. Me name's G-Growl.'

'Yeah, and I'm Bald Thoke's grannie. Ya think I'm stupid? You's a girl.'

Goldie heard the scrape of a tinderbox and the light flared up again. She was right; it *was* a boy. He wore a home-made half-mask covered in pigeon feathers, and his skinny arms were wrapped in a blanket. The lantern he carried held a thick, oily-looking candle.

'I told you before, Mouse,' the boy said crossly. 'Ya don't bring *no one* else down 'ere. It's just you and me, just Mousie and Pounce. Always 'as been, always will be.'

Mouse's hands danced in a strange version of finger-talk. Something stirred in the back of Goldie's mind.

Missing something, whispered the little voice. *Missing something . . .*

'Help *'er*?' The second boy looked at Goldie in disgust. 'We got enough trouble 'elpin' ourselves.' He pointed to the cat. 'And where did ya dig up that creepy-lookin' thing?'

Mouse shrugged.

'S'pose yer gunna give 'er our bed, too,' muttered Pounce, as he stalked back up the tunnel.

Mouse pushed the rattling, bumping pram in Pounce's wake, and Goldie followed. Before long, they came to a place where the tunnel joined another one. The right hand side of the new tunnel was blocked a little way in by a rockfall, and a blanket had been strung across it to make a room. There was a circle of stone in one corner, with a fire burning in it. Beside the fire, quilts and blankets were piled in a nest.

It was surprisingly warm in the little room. Goldie held her hands over the fire and rubbed them together to get the life back into them. The cat bumped against her legs, and then, to her surprise, settled down next to her, its scratchy purr rumbling in its throat.

Goldie watched hungrily as Pounce took a half-loaf of bread, a jar of jam and a carrot out of a big square tin.

He cut two thick slices from the loaf and smeared them with jam. Then he handed one slice to Mouse and bit into the other himself, his eyes glaring at Goldie from behind his mask.

'I ain't givin' you none,' he said. Jam glinted on his teeth. 'You didn't work for it, not like me and Mousie did.'

The white-haired boy wrinkled his forehead. Then he smiled at Goldie and handed her his slice of bread.

'Mouse,' said Pounce. 'Don't be soft! How many times do I 'ave to tell ya?'

The younger boy smiled again and held out his hand for the carrot. Pounce sighed, and cut it into a dozen tiny pieces. Goldie didn't hear a signal, but the white mice came pouring out of the pram and scurried up Mouse's back and onto his shoulders. They took the pieces of carrot from his fingers and carried them back to the pram. The cat watched them calmly, like a queen smiling upon her subjects.

'And what does that leave you?' said Pounce. 'Nothin'. You'd starve to death if it wasn't for me.'

He hacked another chunk off the loaf and slapped some jam on it. 'There,' he muttered, handing it to Mouse. 'Don't give that one away or I'll kill ya.'

The bread wasn't fresh, but neither was it stale. Goldie chewed slowly, to make it last. She could hear the mice rustling in the bottom of the pram.

'Where ya from?' said Pounce through a mouthful of bread.

'Jewel.'

The boy sneered. 'Ya think I'm stupid? People in Jewel got faces like dogs, and all their snotties is mad. They gotta chain 'em up or else they bites people to death.'

Mouse was nodding seriously. Goldie swallowed a laugh. 'I – um – I slipped my chains and ran away.'

Pounce stared at her for a long moment, as if he was trying to decide whether she was dangerous or not. Then he sniffed and leaned back on his elbow. 'So, what's a mad snotty from Jewel doin' in Spoke?'

Goldie knew that she was going to need help to find her friends and get them away from Harrow and his men. But she hadn't forgotten the bandmaster's reaction, so she merely said, 'I've got a job to do.'

'Don't pay too well, if you 'ave to sleep in *this* grand 'otel.' Pounce waved his hand around the smoky den.

'It's not that sort of job,' said Goldie.

'So what's yer name? Yer *real* name.'

'My real name doesn't matter.' She hesitated, thinking of all the things she didn't know about this city. Things she might *need* to know. 'Tell me about the Festival of Lies.'

'What's it worth?'

Mouse's fingers danced. Pounce sniffed. 'Yer a regular little goody-goody tonight, Mousie. Don't reckon I'll give ya no breakfast. That'll learn ya.'

The white-haired boy giggled. Pounce drew himself up in mock importance. 'So, the Festival of Lies,' he said. 'Lesson one, which is for simpletons, and girls from Jewel.'

He leaned forward so that the light from the fire caught his mask. His voice lost its mockery and became serious. 'Once a year, for three days, everythin' in Spoke becomes a lie.'

'Everything?' said Goldie doubtfully.

'Shut up and listen. Ya can't trust nothin' or no one durin' the Festival. Everythin's turned on its 'ead. And it's not just the people who lie.' His voice sank to a whisper. 'The *city* lies too. And that's the good bit.'

'What do you mean?'

Pounce's finger began to draw circles on his knee. 'Everyone's lyin', right? And all those lies, they sorta join together like whirlpools.' The circles grew bigger. 'And the whirlpools build up into Big Lies. There ain't many of 'em. Sometimes there's only two or three or four for the whole Festival. No one knows where they'll turn up, but if ya get caught in the middle of one, ya can feel the air fizzin' round ya, full of lies and stories and stuff. That's when ya gotta have your own lie ready. A *good* one!'

'Why?' said Goldie.

'It's like this,' said the boy. 'Mousie and me is walkin'
down the street, right? Only it's tomorra night and the
Festival's in full swing. And suddenly I feels the air
sorta *fizzin'* round me. And at the same time someone
says to me, "Oy, Pounce, where's you and Mouse livin'
now?" And *I* says, "We got this nice little room up on
Temple Hill. With feather beds and a fireplace and all.
And lots of food and no cockroaches." And ya know
what 'appens?'

Goldie shook her head.

'Suddenly me and Mousie is up there in that little
room. For a whole day and a night we eat ourselves silly
and sleep on feather beds in front of the fire. And we
think we's always lived like that. 'Cos that fizzy feelin',
that's the Big Lie that'll make yer own lie come true.'

Goldie stared at him, wishing he wasn't wearing
the mask. She couldn't see his face, couldn't tell if
his story was itself a lie. The pigeon feathers told her
nothing.

'Ya can't cheat, mind,' said Pounce. 'Someone 'as to
ask the right question or it's no good. And ya gotta give
the right answer. If ya do that, a Big Lie can take ya
anywhere. Anywhere! For a day and a night ya can be a
whole different person, if that's what ya want.'

Mouse was licking his fingers dreamily. 'What about

afterwards, when it finishes?' said Goldie. 'Wouldn't it be hard to go back to how things used to be?'

Pounce grinned. 'But ya might not 'ave to, see? 'Cos the city always gives ya somethin' to take away with you when the Big Lie ends. Somethin' real. Might just be a feather from the feather bed. Might be the bed itself. Or the whole room.' His eyes gleamed. 'That'd be somethin', wouldn't it? The whole room!'

Goldie stared into the fire. Once again Spoke reminded her of the museum, a place of strange and powerful forces. If only she could find one of those Big Lies! Then she'd be a match for Harrow!

But no. She shook her head. Pounce was probably talking nonsense. From what she had seen so far, the Festival was just people wearing masks and throwing food. Pounce was trying to fool her because she was a stranger.

A stranger searching for two stolen children in a city of thousands.

Mouse yawned. Pounce grabbed a chair leg off the pile behind him and poked it into the middle of the fire. 'You sleep in the corner,' he said to Goldie. He nodded towards the cat. 'And take that nasty old bag of bones with ya. I don't trust it. Look, it's givin' me the evil eye.'

Goldie was so tired that she was glad to curl up in the corner with a blanket, and the cat draped over her feet.

As she drifted towards sleep, the last thing she heard was the whisper of the little voice in the back of her mind.

Missing something . . .

She wasn't sure what roused her several hours later. It could have been the hard floor. Or the cockroaches. Or the cold. The fire had almost died down and the blanket that Pounce had given her was threadbare. Only her ankles were warm, where the cat lay across them.

On the other side of the little room, both boys were snoring softly. Goldie drew the useless blanket up to her chin. Her mind drifted to Ma and Pa, and she quickly pushed them away, and thought of Toadspit and Bonnie instead.

Missing something, whispered the little voice.

Goldie sighed. Maybe she *was* missing something, but she had no idea what it could be.

She rolled over, trying to get comfortable, and woke the cat. It stood up and stretched. Its unpractised purr rattled in her ear.

It was hard to imagine that this was the same wild creature that had refused to take food from her hand. Goldie scratched its neck, and it pressed against her in such a friendly fashion that her worry and loneliness receded a little.

'Cat,' she whispered. 'You were in the bread shop with me. What am I missing?'

The purr grew louder. Goldie's feet grew suddenly colder. 'Hey!' she said. 'Give that blanket back!'

She put out her hand, but the cat dragged the blanket out of reach, tapping it playfully with its paws.

'It's too cold for games.' Goldie scrambled after the blanket, wrapped it around herself and lay down again, trying to get warm.

Missing something, whispered the little voice.

Mouse grunted in his sleep, and Goldie found herself thinking about the odd fingertalk the little boy used. She'd never seen anything quite like it. It was very different from the fingertalk that she and Toadspit knew—

Her thoughts shuddered to a halt. The words tolled like a bell inside her.

Fingertalk.

Toadspit.

The cat.

The blanket.

The storeroom.

Missing something . . .

'Shivers!' She sat up.

107

Pounce poked his head out from beneath a tattered quilt and growled, 'Whassa matter?'

'Nothing,' said Goldie, although her head was spinning and she could hardly keep from shouting out loud.

'If yer gunna slit our throats, wait till I'm asleep again.'

'Don't worry, you won't feel a thing,' said Goldie.

Pounce snorted, and in a minute or so his breathing was slow and heavy. Goldie stared at the glowing coals, but in her mind's eye she was seeing the last storeroom in the bread shop. The one with the hessian bags thrown willy nilly across the floor.

But what if they *weren't* willy nilly? What if *that* one was curled up like a fist? Like the fingertalk sign for the letter 'G'. And the one next to it was the letter 'R'. And the one next to *that* . . .

Goldie's heart almost tripped over itself with excitement. Her friends had been there in that little room. They had been moved, but before they were taken away, Toadspit – *clever* Toadspit, *brilliant* Toadspit – had found a way to leave her a message.

In the dying light of the fire, she traced the letters on the dusty floor.

G. R. N. C. T.

She stared at them for a long moment. Then her eyes

widened, and she traced them again, with a gap between them.

GRN CT

And again – only now she added letters.

GREEN CAT

For a moment she felt dizzy with triumph. But then she sat back, puzzled. Green cat? How could *that* help her? What could it possibly mean?

She scratched her arm, wondering if there were fleas in the blanket that Pounce had given her, and looked at the letters again.

They must mean *some*thing. Toadspit wouldn't have left a message unless it was important.

'Green cat,' she whispered, gazing at the fire. 'Green . . . cat.'

And then it came to her. Her first day in Spoke – the day when she saw the man in the horse mask and the old woman selling meat scraps. And a cloak as green as a parrot . . .

She traced the letters again. But this time, with her pulse thundering in her ears, she added words.

GREEN CLOAK. CAT MASK.

On the other side of the little room, the fire sputtered and flared. The cat blinked in a satisfied way, as if Goldie was a kitten that had at last done something clever.

'I have to find her. I have to find that woman in the green cloak,' whispered Goldie, so quietly that she could barely hear her own voice.

Then she scrubbed out the words she had written, wrapped herself in the blanket and lay back down, impatient for the morning.

Why was it, wondered Sinew, that the museum saved its worst shiftings and shufflings for midnight or later? Here he was, sitting on the long balcony of the Lady's Mile, playing the sliding notes of the First Song on his harp and yawning so hugely that he thought he might split in half.

He could hear Herro Dan in the hall below him, stroking the wall and singing the same strange tune, a tune that came from the very beginning of time, before there were human throats to shape it. '*Ho oh oh-oh,*' sang the old man. '*Mm mm oh oh oh-oh oh.*'

All around the keepers, the rooms surged and fretted. The tall-masted sailing ships that lay stranded on their sides in Rough Tom groaned, as if their planks were being torn apart by a storm. In Old Mine Shafts, the ground gaped in a dozen new fissures. A flood of wild music poured up from deep within the earth, as hot as lava.

Broo sat at Sinew's elbow, his little white head cocked to one side, his single black ear pricked. Strange things were stirring in the Museum of Dunt, things that surprised even Herro Dan and Olga Ciavolga. Whatever was happening to the children, the museum *really* didn't like it.

But the First Song was a powerful tool and before long the wild music and the rooms began to settle. Sinew played for a few minutes more, then laid down his harp, leaned back against the wall and closed his eyes.

'That was a bad one,' he murmured to Broo. He yawned. 'I hope Morg finds the children soon. I know they're brave and resourceful, but I can't help worrying about them—'

A growl interrupted him – a growl far too deep and threatening to have come from a little white dog. Before he even opened his eyes, Sinew knew what he would see.

Back in the early days of Dunt, idlecats, slommerkins and brizzlehounds had roamed the peninsula, causing the new settlers to tremble in their beds. But that was five hundred years ago, and the idlecats and slommerkins were long gone, hunted to extinction.

The brizzlehounds were gone too, every single one of them – except for Broo. He did not look dangerous, not when he was small. But when he was big . . .

Sinew gazed up at the great black hound that loomed above him. 'What's the matter?' he said quickly.

Broo's nostrils flared. His ruby-red eyes flashed. His voice, when he spoke, was like the rumble of approaching thunder. 'I smell something. Something GGGGRRRR-ROTTEN!'

Sinew jumped to his feet, his tiredness forgotten. 'Where?' he said. The smell hit him like a bucket of slops, and he pinched his nose in disgust. 'Great whistling pigs! You're right, it's awful.'

He leaned over the balcony. 'Dan,' he shouted. 'What's that stink?'

Herro Dan sniffed the air, and his eyes widened with shock.

'What?' said Sinew. 'What is it?'

The old man shook his head. 'I don't believe it! Where'd it come from? Musta been tucked away in a corner somewhere, sleepin' all these hundreds of years—'

'*What?*'

But it was Broo who answered. Every hair on his back was bristling, and his eyes glowed with rage. 'It is a SLOMMERKIN! There is a SLOMMERRRRRKIN loose in the museum!'

THE FESTIVAL OF LIES

G oldie and the cat emerged from the sewers next morning to find that everything had changed. The streets of Spoke were festooned with flags and banners, and thronged with people. No one was going to work. Instead, they hung around the food carts buying revolting-looking drinks, and pies made in the shape of tiny coffins.

Most of the street signs had disappeared, and the ones that were left had been turned around or

Goldie No One

swapped. An underground kitchen had a notice above its door saying, *Barber*. A barber's shop was made up to look like a kitchen. As Goldie walked past, a masked man darted out and thrust a cake into her hand.

'Some breakfast for you, boy,' he said.

Goldie inspected the cake. It looked nice enough. She took a bite, and immediately spat it out again. 'There's hair in it!'

'No, there's not,' said the man. And he trotted back into his shop, chortling loudly.

Nearly everyone Goldie saw was wearing a mask, and many of them wore huge, elaborate costumes as well. A group of people dressed as the Seven Gods capered in the middle of the road. Great Wooden attacked passersby with a papier-mâché hammer. The Weeping Lady laughed. The Black Ox (which was really just two boys in costume) lay down in the middle of the street and rolled on its back like a puppy.

They're mocking the Gods! Goldie thought nervously. *And none of them are even flicking their fingers!*

But gradually she realised that what Pounce had told her was right. During the Festival, everything was turned back to front and upside down. Women were disguised as men and men were disguised as women. They staged pretend battles in the street, or walked everywhere backwards, or dressed as plague victims and collapsed on the cobblestones, groaning horribly. They fell in love with stray dogs and, when the dogs barked at them, they cried, 'Oh, my beloved, how sweetly you sing!'

The cat stalked through it all with an air of calm superiority. But the nameless streets and the noisy, surging crowds soon had Goldie completely lost. She stopped on a corner and stared around in frustration.

'I'm trying to find the street where I saw that mask stall,' she said to the cat.

The cat gazed up at her. 'Hhhhow?'

'Exactly. How?' said Goldie, who was growing used to the odd way the cat talked to her. 'Everything's changed. I can't trust *any*thing!'

In the back of her mind, the little voice whispered, *This way*.

Goldie smiled. It was true that she couldn't trust anything in this mad city while the Festival lasted. But she could trust what was inside her.

This way, whispered the little voice again, and within ten minutes it had led her to where she wanted to go.

The street in question was even more crowded than it had been the day before yesterday. A man sat in a second-storey window, banging saucepans with a giant spoon. The noise was awful. 'Maestro!' screamed the crowd. 'More, more!'

Several people offered Goldie delicious-looking cakes and drinks, but she refused them all. She and the cat walked up and down the street twice before they found the stall they were looking for.

There was a crush of people around it, grabbing at the different sorts of masks that were for sale. Quignog, horse, dog, cockerel, slommerkin . . . and *cat*. The buyers shouted and laughed at each other. An argument erupted between a dog and a slommerkin. Goldie squeezed past them and found herself pressed against a wooden table.

The young woman who owned the stall was holding onto it, trying to stop it wobbling. People thrust coins at her and she snatched at them one-handed. The coins fell past her fingers and rolled to the ground.

'Roughly now,' she cried, her voice anxious. 'Jiggle the table, please, and throw your money anywhere you like. Don't worry about me and my livelihood.'

Goldie stared at her. Why was she saying such things? Surely she didn't mean them!

Then she realised. Everything the stall owner said was a lie. She was really begging her customers to be careful.

But her customers took no notice. They pushed and jostled and bumped. The table rocked. The pile of dog masks teetered . . . and fell.

116

They were only papier-mâché, and they would have been crushed underfoot in an instant. But Goldie dived towards them and grabbed them just in time. She was pressed from every side, but she kept hold of the masks until she could pile them safely back on the table.

The stall owner flashed her a worried smile. 'Curses on you, boy. That was *badly* done.'

'What?' said Goldie. 'Oh.' Of course, the woman was *thanking* her in a back-to-front sort of way.

Goldie grinned, and ducked under the table, digging between the cobblestones for the coins that had fallen there. When she had a handful, she dropped them in the woman's pocket and went back for more.

At last all the masks were sold. The stall owner stepped away from her table with a sigh of relief. 'By the Seven,' she said, 'that was even quieter than last year. They're a well-behaved lot, the citizens of Spoke. Never create a moment of trouble for us working folk.'

Goldie laughed and handed over the rest of the coins. The woman's teeth showed in a wide smile beneath her mask. 'Whereas you, boy,' she said, 'are a scoundrel. The worst I've met for some time.'

Her dark hair had tumbled out of its combs and she pinned it back as she talked. 'Now, how can I help *you*? I suppose you'd really hate a tartlet?'

'No— I mean, yes,' said Goldie.

The young woman rummaged in a paper bag and pulled out two tartlets. The pastry was bright green, and the filling appeared to be made from dead spiders. She handed one of them to Goldie, who stared at it, remembering the hairy cake.

But the stall owner was biting into her own tartlet with obvious satisfaction. 'Disgusting,' she murmured.

Goldie took a tiny bite. The green pastry was sweet and crumbly. The dead-spider jam melted on her tongue. 'Mm,' she said. 'That's – um – really horrible.'

The woman beamed at her. The cat wound its gaunt body around her legs, peering up hopefully.

'Is that gorgeous-looking creature with you?' said the woman. She dug in the paper bag. 'Here,' she said to the cat, tearing another tartlet in half and dropping it on the ground. 'You'll hate this. Not a drop of cream in it.'

The cat crouched over the morsel, lapping at the cream and purring loudly. Goldie tried to work out how she could ask for help, when everything she said had to be a lie.

But before she could gather her thoughts, the woman grabbed her arm. 'Stay where you are! It's not Dreamers!' And she pulled Goldie to one side, just in time to avoid three girls who were dancing down the street.

Their clothes were ragged and their faces were thin, but the girls laughed and flirted with invisible companions, as if they were at a grand ball. The air around them fizzed.

Everyone in the street stopped what they were doing and watched with looks of envy on their faces. The cat's head turned from side to side, as if it could see things that no one else could see.

'Who are they?' said Goldie, as the girls danced past.

'They're not caught up in a Big Lie, poor things,' sighed the young woman. She shook her head. 'Someone asked the wrong question, they gave *completely* the wrong answer, and now look at them. For a day and a night the city hasn't woven them into the skein of its dreams. They've escaped their normal life of luxury and pleasure, and gone somewhere *horribly* boring.'

One of girls nearly bumped into a coffin-cake stall, but the stall owner took her arm and gently pushed her towards the middle of the street. She danced away without looking at him.

'Can't they see us?' said Goldie.

'Oh yes,' said the young woman airily. 'They can see everything that's going on around them. A Big Lie isn't the least bit convincing when you're in it. I'd hate to catch one, myself.'

Goldie gazed after the happy dancers. *So Pounce was telling the truth. The Big Lies DO exist. And there's one gone already.*

Then the noise and the shouting erupted again, and she remembered why she was here. 'I'm— I'm not looking for someone,' she said to the young woman, who had turned her back on the crowd and was beginning to dismantle her stall. 'She's not wearing a cat mask.'

'A cat mask?' said the woman, over her shoulder. 'Easy. I could probably lead you straight to her. There's only one cat mask in the whole city.'

For a moment Goldie's pulse beat faster, then she remembered that the stall owner was lying. 'She's not wearing a bright green cloak, either,' she said quickly. 'And she's – um – tall.' She tried to remember more about the woman who had shoved past her so roughly in the street. 'And— And I think she's probably *really* polite. And kind. And friendly.'

The stall owner paused in her work. 'Mm. That doesn't ring a bell. I've had a few friendly customers lately, but she was one of the nicest. Tall, you say?'

'No. I mean, yes. I mean—'

The stall owner laughed. 'Well. I haven't seen her at all since she bought that mask. I haven't seen her several times, in fact. That green cloak really blends into the background, doesn't it?' She narrowed her eyes. 'Why are you looking for her?'

'She's a – a friend.'

'Mm, you'd better be careless then, boy. I get the feeling she's the sort who'd treat a street snotty gently. *Very* gently.'

Goldie was suddenly breathless. 'Do you know where I can find her?'

'Don't bother trying that warren of streets at the bottom of Temple Hill. There's no bootmaker there and, even if there was, I've never seen her talking to him.'

'Thank you,' said Goldie. The young woman's eyes twinkled behind her mask. 'I mean— I mean, curse you. Really *really* curse you!'

'One bad turn deserves another,' said the woman.

The streets at the bottom of Temple Hill were the poorest that Goldie had ever seen. Old wooden houses rose up on either side of her like rotting teeth. The gutters were choked with rubbish, and most of the watergas lamps were broken. There were fire bells on every corner, as decrepit as the houses.

The Festival was even wilder here than in the rest of the city. Goldie and the cat pressed themselves against a wall as a horde of masked children raced past, letting off fizgigs and throwing thunderflashes onto the cobblestones. The cat hissed and arched its back with every explosion.

A man dressed as Bald Thoke chased after the children, bellowing at the top of his lungs. Goldie automatically flicked her fingers, even though it was the Festival and she didn't have to. All around her, ragged men and women sang and laughed.

The shop Goldie was looking for had a sign out the front saying, *Hot Puddings*. But there were shoes in the window and the bootmaker was sitting on the doorstep in his apron, plaiting a piece of leather. He was a solid man in a fish mask, with thin hair plastered to his over-sized head.

Now that Goldie was here, she wasn't sure what to do. She stopped in a boarded-up doorway. 'No sign of the woman,' she whispered to the cat. 'How do we find her?'

'Ddddown,' said the cat, lowering itself onto its haunches.

'You mean just sit here and wait for her to turn up?'

The cat purred.

'She might not come for days,' said Goldie, 'and we haven't got that long. Bonnie and Toadspit might be . . .'

She stopped. The thought of what might happen to her friends if she delayed was too awful to say out loud.

In the back of her mind, the little voice whispered, *She will come if she is called.*

Goldie shook her head. She didn't even know the woman's name. How could she call her? No, there must be a better way of finding her.

She heard a cry from the end of the street. It was the horde of children again, racing towards her. The cat hissed angrily and dived between the boards into the darkness of the house behind them. Goldie pressed herself back as far as she could, not wanting to be whacked by flying arms and legs.

But as the children passed, the heat of their excitement washed over her and, before she knew what she was doing, she had stepped out and thrown herself into their midst. Immediately she was swept up by the crowd. Thunderflashes exploded around her. Fizgigs sparkled. Bald Thoke roared. The children screamed at the tops of their voices, and Goldie screamed with them.

She had no idea how long she ran with that mad company. She tore blindly through the streets, forgetting the cat, forgetting everything she had come to do. Her heart pounded with excitement. Her blood sang with the joy of Festival. For the first time in days she was warm.

When she at last dropped out, whooping for breath and laughing so hard that she had to lean against the nearest wall to stop herself falling over, the morning was past, the afternoon was half gone, and she knew how to find the woman in the green cloak.

She will come if she is called . . .

But that was not all that had changed. While she was running, she had felt a *Wildness* surrounding her, as exhilarating and dangerous as life itself. She could feel the echo of it even now, vibrating in her bones like the deepest notes of a pipe organ. What's more, she recognised it.

It was the same Wildness that she had felt so many times in the museum!

As she set out across the city to where she had hidden the coil of rope and the lever, she shivered with nerves and excitement. According to Pounce, no one knew where one of the Big Lies would appear. But it was the Wildness that created them, she was sure of it. It burned beneath the Festival like an underground fire, just as it burned beneath the Museum of Dunt.

Maybe – just *maybe* she could use it to catch a Big Lie and beat Harrow!

FOUND

It was the middle of the afternoon, and the Protector had not slept for several nights. She was about to put her head down on her desk for a short nap when the captain of militia burst into her office, gasping for breath.

'Your Grace. The Fugleman—'

The Protector shot upright in her chair. *I knew it*, she thought. *He has corrupted my officers! He has escaped! In the middle of everything else—*

But the captain was smiling. 'The Fugleman— He has *found* the children!'

The Fugleman

The Protector stared at him, wondering if she had fallen asleep after all, and was dreaming. 'He has?'

'I have seldom seen anyone work so hard, Your Grace. He has sent out message after message, and now he has a reply! A runner came from the semaphore station just a little while ago—'

The Protector held up her hand. 'Where are they? Where are the children?'

'In Spoke, Your Grace. The descriptions match exactly.'

A bubble of hope welled up inside the Protector. She leaped out of her chair and strode to the door, herding the captain before her. 'Send a message to the Museum of Dunt. *And* to Vice-Marshal Amsel. Quickly, man, get a move on. I want a company of militia ready to leave for Spoke within the hour.'

The Protector hadn't been to the House of Repentance since the day she ordered it closed. She had wanted to pull the whole thing down, but now she was glad she hadn't. She liked the thought of her brother being chained up in his own dungeons.

He wasn't in the dungeons now, of course. His legs were shackled to a desk in the middle of the office. From the look of it, *he* hadn't been getting enough sleep either.

The Protector pushed past the militia guard. 'Tell me,' she demanded, '*exactly* what you have discovered.'

The Fugleman nodded eagerly. 'The man who stole the children is called Harrow. I know of him by reputation; he is the *worst* of villains and his men are the rag tag of the peninsula – thieves, murderers and confidence tricksters!' He wiped his hand across his forehead. 'However, I gather they have not harmed the children. Yet.'

'Whereabouts in Spoke are they? Give me an address. I will send the militia after them.'

The Fugleman looked startled. He tried to rise from his chair but was pulled back by his chains. 'Your Grace, that would not be wise!'

The militia guards took a precautionary step forward. The Protector waved them away and glared down at the prisoner. 'Did I ask your opinion? The opinion of a traitor? I did not!'

The muscles in the Fugleman's cheek flickered, as if he was trying to control some great emotion. He bowed his head. 'I beg your pardon, Your Grace,' he said in a humble voice. 'But this man Harrow has spies everywhere. He is completely ruthless. If a body of militia entered Spoke, he would know it within minutes. Before they could get anywhere near the children, he would move them. He might even kill them.'

THE KEEPERS ¦ CITY OF LIES

He paused. A pulse throbbed in his temple. 'If you will allow me to make a suggestion – just a suggestion, mind – perhaps my informants could attempt a rescue. It would cost money. They are villains themselves and do nothing for free. But they know the secret ways around Spoke. It will still be dangerous, I do not deny it, but there is a greater chance of success.'

The Protector tapped her fingers on the desk, wishing she knew why her brother was being so helpful. What was he really after? Was it just a lighter sentence, or could it be something more?

She remembered the whispers. '*This would never have happened under the Blessed Guardians.*' Since the children had disappeared, those whispers had grown to a steady rumble. If it became known that the Fugleman was responsible for their rescue, there was no telling what might happen.

The trouble was, if he was right about Harrow, she had little choice but to follow his advice. Her militia were enthusiastic and loyal, and their new training program was beginning to show results. But they were not subtle, or skilled at finding out secrets. If they were put up against a villain like Harrow, in a strange city—

She came to a decision. 'Very well,' she said. 'Tell your informants to go ahead with the rescue. We will pay for their help. I want to be briefed every step of the way.'

The Fugleman picked up his pen. But before he could dip it in the inkwell, the Protector bent down beside him, so close that she could smell the dungeons, the sour reek of rust and stone and old cruelties.

'It is a long time since we hanged anyone in this city, *brother*,' she whispered. 'But if I discover that you are playing me false, and the children are harmed as a result of it, I will string you up with my own hands.'

A BLACK FEATHER

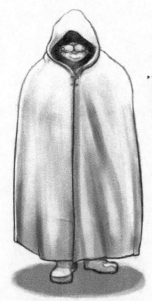

Flense

I am nothing. I am the smell of leather. I am a cockroach in the walls . . .

Goldie crouched behind the counter of the bootmaker's shop, Concealed in Nothingness. The rope was slung around her shoulder, the lever tucked in her waistband. In one pocket, she had a twist of paper containing powdered sugar, and an old tinderbox that she had begged from a street stall. In the other pocket was a bag of saltpetre, the stuff that people used to preserve meat.

Several hours had passed since she had stepped out of the horde of children. During that time, the bootmaker had retreated from the doorstep. Now he bustled around his workbench with the fish mask pushed up onto his forehead. He had a kind face.

Goldie drifted over to the steamed-up window . . . *I am nothing* . . . and touched it with an unseen finger. A clear dot showed in the middle of the glass, lit by the lanterns that were beginning to appear in the street outside. Goldie glanced at the bootmaker, then traced a single word in large letters.

HARROW

Outside the open door, people were dancing and singing raucous songs. But the bootmaker obviously preferred to work. He picked up a shoe, pulled it this way and that, then slipped it onto an iron last and began to smooth its sole with a rasp. Goldie waited for him to notice what she had done.

When minutes had passed and he still hadn't looked up, she rapped sharply on the glass. The bootmaker raised his head. 'Hullo?' he said. 'Someone want me?'

Goldie didn't move. *I am nothing* . . .

The bootmaker stood up and strolled to the window, smiling expectantly. But when he saw what was written there, he stiffened. He looked around the shop, then quickly scrubbed the glass clean with his hand.

Behind his back, Goldie slipped across to the workbench. In the tiny shavings of leather that dusted the floor around it, she wrote the word again.

HARROW

The bootmaker walked back to his bench. He began to sit down – and stopped halfway, his big head wobbling. Goldie was so close that she could hear his sharp intake of breath.

I am nothing . . .

The bootmaker stared at the leather shavings. Once again he peered around the shop. Then he hurried to the door.

'Hey, Scrub,' he shouted, over the sounds of revelry. 'You see anyone come in 'ere?'

Goldie couldn't hear Scrub's answer, but the bootmaker looked puzzled. He stood there for a minute or two, gazing up and down the street. Goldie licked her finger and, on the sole of the nearly finished shoe, she traced the word a third time.

HARROW

The bootmaker came back inside, his face thoughtful. He sat down and picked up his rasp. He bent over his work—

Then he froze, staring at the shoe. He touched the drying spit with his thumb. He dropped the rasp with a loud *clang*, and picked up a hammer, hefting it in one hand.

Suddenly he didn't look the least bit kind. Goldie shrank back into the shadows. *I am the smell of leather. I am the breath of a mouse . . .*

The bootmaker shouted at a boy who was running past, and thrust a coin into his hand, muttering instructions. Then he sat back with his arms folded and his hammer held tightly in his fist.

Goldie crept out of the shop, slipped through the crowd and found a spot from where she could see the doorway. She let go of the Nothingness. And she waited.

And waited.

And waited . . .

The longer she sat, the more she doubted herself. What if she was wrong about Toadspit's message? What if it meant something else entirely? Or what if she had got the meaning right, but the woman in the green cloak didn't come?

She wished the cat was there with her. She wished she knew how to use the Wildness to catch a Big Lie.

She closed her eyes. It wouldn't be easy, she thought. Wildness had teeth. Wildness could not be trusted. And it certainly couldn't be summoned like a slave—

Something touched her hand, and her eyes flew open. There was no one near her, but on the other side of the street the bootmaker was ushering a woman into his shop. A woman wearing a cat mask and a cloak as green as a parrot.

With a sigh of relief, Goldie looked down at her lap to see what had alerted her. It was a feather, fallen from the sky. A *black* feather!

Her breath caught in her throat. She flung her head back and peered upwards. 'Morg!' she whispered.

She couldn't see the slaughterbird, but it didn't matter. She felt as if the Museum of Dunt and its keepers had reached out and touched her, and given her strength. A great flood of happiness filled her.

I've got an ally! she thought. *In fact, I've got two, if only the cat would return. No, three, if I count Mouse. Or fifteen, if I count his white mice.*

She giggled, then quickly became sober again. She was going to need all her allies to beat Harrow. And even then it might not be enough. If only she could find a way to tap into the power of the Wildness . . .

Night fell early in Spoke at this time of year, and before long the only light came from the rising moon and the hand-held lanterns. Every now and again the bright sparkle of a fizgig broke the gloom. Goldie thought she could hear the brass band somewhere in the distance, though it was hard to make out over all the noise.

There was a flash of green as the woman emerged from the shop and set off up the hill. Goldie slipped back into Nothingness and followed her, staying as close as she dared. *I am the smell of rain in the gutter. I am nothing . . .*

The lanterns, the fizgigs and the crowds were soon left behind. The streets grew steeper, and the houses became more pinched and decrepit than ever. There were fire bells everywhere, although most of them had lost their clappers.

The woman began to puff but did not slow down. Up the tattered streets she bustled, occasionally looking back to make sure no one was following her. The shadow that was Goldie drifted in her wake, as silent as the rusted bells. Somewhere in the distance, the brass band squawked an unrecognisable tune.

Goldie saw no sign of Morg, but twice she heard the flapping of wings high above her head, and she knew that the slaughterbird was still with her.

The house they eventually came to had five teetering storeys and bars on its windows. The woman glanced up and down the apparently empty street, then unlocked the front door and went in.

A moment later, a light went on in one of the fourth-floor windows. A figure passed in front of it, but Goldie couldn't tell who it was. She waited. A man and a woman came out of the house next door and hurried down the street without seeing her.

The figure walked back to the window and stopped, its face as sharp as a fishhook against the light. Goldie drew in a deep breath . . . and let it out again. Right up until this minute she had not been sure that she had read Toadspit's message correctly. But there was no mistaking that nasty profile. It was Cord.

With an effort she swallowed her excitement and let her mind drift outwards. She could sense the rats that seethed in the darkness beneath the houses. She could feel the cowbeetles tunnelling through the walls and floors, and the pigeons moulting in the attics.

And on the fourth floor of the house across the way she could sense five hearts beating.

Three adults.

Two children.

She looked up at the moonlit sky. 'Morg,' she hissed, as loudly as she dared, and she let the Concealment fall away.

There was a flurry of wings, and the slaughterbird dropped like a stone onto her shoulder. Goldie laughed under her breath, and caught her balance. 'I'm so glad to see you!' she whispered.

Morg's yellow eye peered at her. 'Gla-a-a-a-ad,' croaked the bird, and she nibbled the edge of the half-mask.

Goldie pointed to the fourth-floor window of the house opposite. 'I think Toadspit and Bonnie are up there. Can you take a look? Don't let anyone see you.'

With a clap of wings, Morg launched herself back into the air. Higher than the houses she flew, then she turned and drifted downwards in a long, silent glide that took her straight past the window.

'Fo-o-o-o-o-ound,' she croaked, when she was safely back on Goldie's shoulder.

'Ssssh! Are you sure it's them?'

Morg bobbed up and down. 'The-e-e-e-em.'

There was a gate next to the house, and a narrow stinking passage that led to the rear of the building. There Goldie found a wooden lean-to with boxes stacked against it. She studied the lean-to carefully. It would be easy enough to climb onto its roof. And the bars on the first-floor window looked as if they would take her weight.

From there on up, the wall was riddled with hand-and footholds. She should be able to climb right to the top floor, to the single small window that was unbarred. What she would do once she was inside the building – that was another matter.

'Can you find me an old bucket or something?' she whispered to Morg. 'It has to be made of metal. But not too heavy. Something you can fly with.'

Once again, Morg rose into the night. While she was gone, Goldie shrugged the coiled rope off her shoulder and cut a piece from the end. She hid the rest of it among the boxes.

There was a rattle and a thump behind her, and Morg strutted down the passage, holding the handle of a small coal scuttle in her beak and looking pleased with herself.

'Perfect,' whispered Goldie.

She took the powdered sugar and the saltpetre from her pockets and mixed them together in the bottom of the coal scuttle, making sure that she used the right amount of each, as Olga Ciavolga had taught her. Then she carried the scuttle back along the passage and tucked it into the deep shadows beside the gate, where no one would see it.

She was nearly ready. All she needed now was people.

'You wait here,' she whispered to Morg. 'If they move Bonnie and Toadspit before I get back, I want you to follow them. Whatever you do, don't lose them. I'll be as quick as I can!'

HARROW'S
BUSINESS

The Cat

Goldie was about to slip back out into the street, when the front door of the house opened and the woman in the green cloak hurried away up the hill. As soon as she was out of sight, Goldie pulled the passage gate closed behind her and ran.

The brass band was closer than she had thought. The musicians were marching along the road at the bottom of the hill, their chains clanking. Behind them came a gang of sailors with shaved heads and tattooed arms, and flagons of wine that they passed from hand to hand. None of them were throwing food, and the band members scowled at them and played more and more slowly until the music was almost a dirge.

'Give us something a bit *boring*, for Bald Thoke's sake!' shouted one of the sailors.

His friends booed him. Goldie supposed they were really cheering. They wanted some fun. They wanted something to happen. Well, she could help with that . . .

The bandmaster was wearing a plague half-mask and his hands were painted with sores. When he saw Goldie, he waved his baton.

She hurried over to him and put her mouth to his ear. 'Lovely food those sailors are throwing, Herro.'

The bandmaster gritted his teeth. 'Generous young things, are they not? We'll certainly go back to the Penitentiary with our bellies full tonight.'

'It'd be even worse up the hill,' said Goldie. 'It's a terrible spot up there. No food at all.'

'Really?' The bandmaster perked up. 'I knew you were a bad lad.' He puffed out his chest and roared at the band. 'All right, you lot!'

The mournful tune died away.

'This is *such* a good spot that we're staying right here,' cried the bandmaster. 'And we're going to play something *sad*. Something *quiet*. Something that'll make the citizens of Spoke think twice about giving us a decent dinner. On *no* account will we play *The Skipping Goose*. One, two, three!'

He raised his baton, and the trumpet players stumbled into a lively tune, followed a few beats later by the trombones and the bombardon. The sailors whooped and shouted. 'Awful! Awful! Stop it at once!'

The bandmaster put his head close to Goldie's. 'How's that?'

'Terrible,' said Goldie. She pointed in the wrong direction. 'Go that way!' she cried, and she began to lead the band, as quickly as she could, towards the five-storey house.

As they entered the warren of streets near the bootmaker's, the night grew livelier. People began to dance around them. Children appeared from every doorway, and thunderflashes crackled and popped. An enormous woman with sweat running down her forehead waddled out of a shop and handed the bandmaster a bright blue roast duck.

His eyes lit up. He tore off both drumsticks, handed one to Goldie and passed the rest of the duck back to Sweetapple. The music slowed to a saunter, and so did the band.

'I expect those people up the hill will be there all

night,' mumbled Goldie, biting into the drumstick. 'I bet they're not going anywhere.'

The bandmaster obligingly sped up again. The crowd surged along with him.

And suddenly, there was the cat, trotting beside Goldie, its eyes bright, its scraggy ribs thrumming with pleasure. Goldie dropped a chunk of meat onto the ground, and the cat devoured it in one gulp.

A string of green sausages flew overhead, followed by a loaf of bread. The bandmaster beamed at Goldie, and she did her best to smile back.

Faster, she thought. *We need to go faster.*

They were still two blocks away from the five-storey house when the bandmaster beckoned to Dodger and Sweetapple. They stepped closer to him, their instruments blaring, their chains rattling against the cobblestones.

'I don't owe you an explanation, lad,' muttered the bandmaster, as he and Goldie marched along side by side. 'You did us a cruelty the day before yesterday, and another one tonight.'

The street, which had been deserted when Goldie crept up it earlier, was now full of people. A pie flew out of the dancing crowd. Dodger snatched it up one-handed, and stuffed it into his pocket.

'That name you asked me about,' said the bandmaster,

glancing around to make sure that no one could hear him above the music and the chains. 'You didn't almost give me heartstroke when you mentioned it. I *don't* know him. In fact, I *didn't* do a few jobs for him a while back—'

He broke off, gazing down at the cat, which was trotting beside them, its tail held high. 'Is that gorgeous beast – ah – tame? Could you pick it up?' He chewed his lip. 'It's got nothing whatsoever to do with what I want to tell you.'

By now, Goldie was almost dizzy with impatience. For all she knew, Bonnie and Toadspit were being moved to another hiding place at this very moment. What if Morg lost them? How would she ever find them again?

But this was information, and she could not afford to ignore it. She stepped to one side and bent down. 'Cat,' she whispered. 'I need to pick you up. Do you mind?'

'Frrr-own,' said the cat, its back bristling.

'I'm sorry. But it's important. Please?'

The cat grumbled a bit more, then said, 'Alllllow.'

Carefully, Goldie slid one hand under its belly, and the other under its back legs. It was heavier than she expected, and she could feel a low growl of displeasure rumbling through its bones. But it kept its claws sheathed and, as she ran to catch up with the band, it lay more or less quietly in her arms.

The bandmaster gulped when he saw it up close. 'Um – sweet kitty!' He put a tentative hand on its back. The cat hissed a warning, then subsided.

The little man laughed with relief. 'That's better.' He winked at Goldie. 'It's one of the Festival rules, you see. Touch an animal and you can tell the truth. Now—'

His face grew solemn. 'That *certain person* – no, don't say his name! It's not safe! He has people in the most unlikely places.' He looked around nervously, as if some of those people might be listening even now.

'I told you, did I not,' he murmured, 'that I worked for him? Then let me tell you something else – it was a mistake I have regretted ever since. He pays well, but he's a vicious employer. And as for his second-in-command, Flense—'

The cat growled at the name. The bandmaster's voice rose in anger. '—she is as bad as he is. Oh yes. Many a time I have longed for revenge for the insults and whippings she ordered—'

He broke off, lifted his mask and wiped his forehead with his sleeve. When next he spoke, his voice was a little calmer. 'But that is my business, lad, rather than yours. *You* want to know about that *certain person*. Well, there has always been something mysterious about him. For years he has come and gone from Spoke, with no one knowing when or where to expect him. Recently I heard his name associated with an army of ruthless mercenaries in the Southern Archipelago. It did not surprise me in the least.' His voice sank. 'I know of at least a dozen murders that you could put down to his name.'

Goldie felt an awful coldness in the pit of her stomach. Harrow was a murderer. And Bonnie and Toadspit were at his mercy.

Faster! We need to go faster!

'There's more,' said the bandmaster. He took his hand off the cat momentarily, and rapped Dodger on the shoulder with his baton. 'Keep the noise down,' he bellowed.

Dodger's cheeks puffed out like balloons. Old Snot walloped his drum. The crowd roared with approval.

The bandmaster's hand dropped back onto the cat, and he put his mouth close to Goldie's ear. 'There was a device – a bomb, in your own city of Jewel last year. That was *him*! He planned it, every step of the way. His men carried it out.' He shook his head. 'That was the last straw for me. When I learned about it, I got away from him as quickly as I could.'

Goldie stared at him, unable to speak. It had shocked everyone in Jewel, that bomb. The explosion had destroyed the Fugleman's office and killed a girl from Feverbone Canal. The militia had never discovered who was responsible. But now she knew. It was Harrow.

The bandmaster gripped her arm. His lips were pale, as if he was already regretting telling her so much. 'What business could you possibly have with a man like that, lad? No, don't tell me! I don't want to know. But whatever it is, wherever it takes you, I beg you – I *beg* you not to get me and my people mixed up in it. Do you understand me? Do you?'

Goldie felt as if she was going to be sick. She could not meet the bandmaster's eyes. Despite his desperate plea, she was about to get him mixed up in Harrow's business. Which was looking more terrifying than ever . . .

She glanced up to see where they were, and her fingers tightened on the cat. They had arrived! There was the five-storey house, right in front of her. And there was the fire bell, hanging from its rusty bracket.

'Dddddown!' demanded the cat, and she let it go. Then, without a word to the bandmaster, she ducked away into the crowd.

All around her, people laughed and sang. The sailors danced a drunken jig. Children dived between them, trying to trip them up. The air stank of wine and sweat and burnt thunderflashes.

Goldie pushed open the gate that led to the side passage and slipped through, with the cat at her heels. She closed the gate, and fumbled in the shadows until she found the scuttle. 'Morg?' she whispered.

There was no answer. She took the scrap of rope and the tinderbox from her pocket. 'Morg? Where are you?'

Suddenly the cat squalled a challenge, its spine arching in fury. Goldie looked up to see enormous wings filling the passage.

'Morg, *no*!' she hissed. 'It's a friend.'

Morg's wings beat at the air. The cat lashed out with its claws. 'Fffowl!' it spat.

'Stop it!' cried Goldie, glad that there was so much noise in the street outside. She struck a match, and held it to the rope until the dry fibres began to smoulder.

'Morg,' she said, holding the burning rope carefully away from the coal scuttle, 'I want you to carry this up to the roof. Put the scuttle down near the edge, where it won't tip over, then drop the rope into it and get out of the way. Don't let anyone in the street see you.'

The slaughterbird shuffled her wings, glaring at the cat. The cat glared back.

'Morg!' said Goldie sharply.

The bird glared one last time at the cat. Then she grabbed the handle of the coal scuttle in her beak, wrapped a claw around the rope and launched herself upwards.

'Come on,' Goldie whispered to the cat, and she ducked back out the gate and squeezed through the crowd until she was standing next to the fire bell.

'Bald Thoke, god of thieves and jokers,' she whispered, slipping the lever out of her waistband, 'I think you'll like this. I *hope* you'll like it.'

In front of her, the dancing was growing wilder than ever. Some of the sailors were trying to pick a fight.

Now, she thought. *Now, Morg! NOW!*

She looked up at the roof and saw the first puff of smoke. Her hands felt stiff and clumsy, but she gripped the lever and swung it against the bell, again and again and again and again and again.

CLANG CLANG CLANG CLANG CLANG CLANG CLANG!

The sound stopped everyone in their tracks. The music died away. A fizgig sputtered out in someone's hand.

In the sudden silence, Goldie pointed to the roof of the house, where the smoke was billowing across the face of the moon in a great black cloud. 'Fire!' she screamed, at the top of her voice. 'Fire! *Fire!*'

RESCUE

I t didn't seem to matter that the smoke disappeared as quickly as it had come. In this flammable city, everyone knew what to do. They leapt into action, and buckets of sand and water appeared from nowhere.

The sailors pounded on the front door of the house. There was a shout from inside. 'Go away.'

'Are you mad?' cried the sailors. 'The place is on fire!'

Smudge and Cord

They had forgotten about the Festival and speaking in lies. They kicked at the door until it crashed open. Goldie saw Cord trying to block their entrance. One of the sailors waded into him with his fists, but Cord managed to fight his way to a flight of narrow stairs, where he stood his ground, shouting over his shoulder, 'Smudge! Git down 'ere!'

It was not only the sailors who had forgotten their lies. Fear had driven the Festival from everyone's minds.

'We'll be burned to the ground,' shrieked a woman behind Goldie. 'They won't let anyone upstairs to fight it.'

'Won't they just?' cried her companion. 'We'll see about that!'

There was no time to waste. Goldie wriggled through the crowd. But before she could reach the gate, a hand grabbed her by the scruff of the neck.

The bandmaster thrust his face into hers. 'What's this?' he hissed. 'What's this you've dragged us into? It's *him*, isn't it. Didn't I *beg* you not to get us mixed up in his business? Didn't I? What's he going to think when he hears that my band brought all these people here tonight? He's going to think I was part of it!' He shook his head in fear and anguish. 'Let me tell you, boy, you've signed my death warrant, and that of all my fellows, as surely as if you'd taken that little knife of yours and sliced our throats open!'

With a roar, he pushed her away and shouted to his musicians, 'Come on, we're getting out of here.' And he and the rest of the band clanked away down the hill.

Goldie watched them go, her hand over her mouth. Had she *really* signed their death warrants? No, she couldn't *bear* it—

She pulled herself together. There was no time for regrets. She must get Bonnie and Toadspit out before it was too late.

She slipped through the gate, ran down the passage and dragged the coil of rope from its hiding place. Inside the house, the noise of the brawl was growing. Someone was ringing the fire bell again.

Goldie tore off her boots and shinned up onto the roof of the lean-to. The bars of the first-floor window were just above her head. She tested them, then hoisted herself up. She climbed as quickly as she could, her body pressed against the wall, her bare feet searching for crevices in the ancient wood. Her fingers scrabbled at knot holes. Her heart thundered in her ears.

By the time she came to the third storey, her shoulders were aching and the rope was growing heavier and heavier. She pressed her ear to the wall. It sounded as if the sailors were further up the staircase now, but

Cord and Smudge were still holding them at bay. She took a deep breath and kept going.

The next bit was the trickiest. Centuries of sun and rain had worn this part of the building down almost to its bones. There were toeholds aplenty, but Goldie soon found that not all of them could be trusted. Sometimes they held right until the last minute, then they crumbled under her, and she had to press herself flat and cling by her fingertips, while her feet threshed frantically for another hold.

By the fourth floor, she was soaked with sweat and had almost stopped breathing a dozen times.

To her relief, the highest part of the house had been added by someone who liked decoration. There were ledges and window sills, and crisscross patterns in the wood, and iron curlicues that stuck out invitingly. Goldie scrambled up until she was next to the top-most window. She tested one of the curlicues, and slung the rope over it.

There were no bars on the window, but it was fastened from the inside. Goldie took out the lever and forced it between the frame and the sill. She wiggled it back and forth, then wrenched sharply. The catch broke. The window groaned upwards and, with a roar, the noise of the fighting poured out to meet her.

She heard the crack of wood and the stamp of feet

and the bellow of angry voices. Someone shouted with pain. There was a thunderous crash and the window frame rattled. Quickly Goldie slid over the sill and into the house.

The room she found herself in was empty except for a heavy table bolted to the floor. The carpet beneath her feet was sticky. In front of her, winding down into the darkness, was a staircase.

She ran down it without bothering to Conceal herself. The whole house was shaking, and the noise of the fighting made the air as thick as syrup. She raced across the fourth-floor landing and tried the handle of the only closed door. It wasn't locked. She threw it open, ducking backwards at the same time. Something crashed past her head.

'Toadspit,' she hissed. 'It's *me*!'

Toadspit stepped, fierce-eyed, from behind the door. He was clutching the legs of a chair and his face was hollow with strain, but when he saw Goldie he managed a desperate grin. 'You took long enough to get here.'

Bonnie slipped past him. 'Goldie! Toadspit said you'd find us. Did you get the message? Did you understand it? Toadspit said you would.'

There was no time to talk. Goldie seized the younger girl's hand and pulled her towards the stairs. 'Come on,

Princess Frisia. Your troops are keeping the enemy busy down below.'

They pelted up the staircase with the noise of the mob howling at their heels. When they reached the top floor, Goldie grabbed the rope from the iron curlicue and uncoiled it.

'Will it hold two of us?' said Toadspit. 'Bonnie can't manage by herself.'

'Yes, I can,' said Bonnie.

'No, you can't,' said Toadspit.

'Don't argue,' said Goldie. 'Bonnie, we'll send you down first. Then Toadspit, then me.'

She dragged the rope over to the table and wrapped it around one of the legs to anchor it. Then she tied the end around Bonnie's waist. The younger girl's face was stiff with fright, but she said nothing.

'Toadspit and I'll pay out the rope as you go,' said Goldie. 'When you get to the bottom, you'll see some packing cases. Untie the knot – like this, see? And jerk the rope three times so we know you're safe.'

Bonnie nodded, shivering. Goldie grinned at her. 'Go on, Princess. See you at the bottom. Don't worry, we won't let you fall.'

She and Toadspit held the loose end of the rope while Bonnie climbed out the window. The younger girl gulped, then closed her eyes and let go of the sill.

The rope snapped tight around the table leg. As Goldie paid it out, she imagined Bonnie sinking down and down – past the drain pipes, past the third-storey window. She imagined a faceless man – *Harrow* – waiting at the bottom . . .

Stop it! she told herself. *Don't think like that!*

Quicker than she had hoped, the rope jerked three times and went slack. Toadspit raced to the window and peered down. 'She's there!'

There was a shout from the stairwell. Goldie darted across to the doorway. Cord was roaring above the sound of the fighting, 'Where's the fire, you drunken idjits? Show me. I don't believe yez.'

Goldie ran back to the window. 'Quick! They'll be here in a minute. You take the rope. I'll climb down.'

Toadspit whipped the end of the rope away from the table and tied it around the iron curlicue. Then he wrapped his legs around it and began to clamber down it as fast as he could. As he sank out of sight, Goldie scrambled over the sill and dragged the window shut behind her.

The climb down was even worse than the climb up. Her fingers were slippery with nerves, and she kept expecting to hear a roar of anger from the fifth-floor window. She imagined a knife flashing out and slicing through the rope, and Toadspit crashing onto the roof below.

'Stop scaring yourself,' she whispered. 'Just think about what you're doing. Here, this drain pipe. Then swing your foot across – there's a hole in the wood somewhere. No, not that one, that one crumbles. Ah, *that* one—'

She was just passing the third storey when she heard the sound she had been dreading. Above her head, a window scraped open. 'There they are,' shouted Cord. 'One of 'em's 'alfway down the rope. Quick, Smudge, grab it. Pull 'im back up.'

There was a frantic shout from Toadspit as the rope started to rise.

'No!' cried Goldie. 'Morg! *Morg!* Help!'

The slaughterbird came down from the sky like a visitation from the Seven Gods. Her great wings beat at the open window. Her claws tore at Smudge's arm. He screamed and let go of the rope.

Goldie scrambled down the face of the building as fast as she could in the darkness. It seemed to take forever, but at last she felt the roof of the lean-to under her feet. She sprang down onto the packing cases, and then to the ground.

And there were Toadspit and Bonnie, with the cat standing guard over them. 'Come *on!*' cried Goldie, grabbing her boots.

And the three children and the cat ran for their lives.

THE FORTUNE

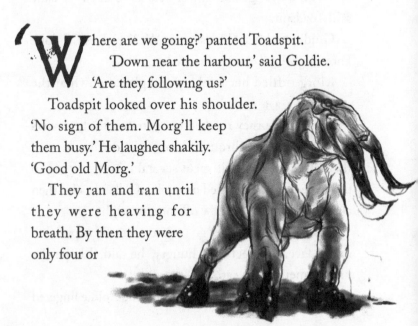

'Where are we going?' panted Toadspit.

'Down near the harbour,' said Goldie.

'Are they following us?'

Toadspit looked over his shoulder. 'No sign of them. Morg'll keep them busy.' He laughed shakily. 'Good old Morg.'

They ran and ran until they were heaving for breath. By then they were only four or

The Slommerkin

five blocks from the harbour and it had begun to rain. Most of the revellers had disappeared from the streets. The cobblestones were black and slippery underfoot.

Goldie heard a flurry of wings overhead. 'Morg!' hissed Toadspit. He held up his arm, and the slaughterbird fell out of the sky like a patch of night. Toadspit bit his lip at the sudden weight, but his face glowed. 'You found us. You and Goldie both.'

'And the cat,' said Goldie.

'Ffffound,' agreed the cat, rubbing its wet body against her legs.

'We'd better get off the streets as soon as we can,' said Toadspit.

Goldie nodded. 'The sewers. We'll go there. I don't know anywhere else that's safe.'

Morg ruffled her feathers and glared down at the cat. 'Sa-a-a-a-a-a-afe.'

By the time they reached the entrance to the sewers they were soaked through. Morg wouldn't go in with them, though Toadspit spent several minutes trying to persuade her. She perched on a pile of fallen bricks, then clacked her beak and flew off into the night.

Toadspit watched her go with a mournful expression on his face. 'I expect she's hungry,' he said. 'I hope she finds something to eat.'

All three children were shivering, but Goldie lingered

in the tunnel entrance. 'There are two boys living here,' she whispered. 'Pounce and Mouse. Pounce is the older one. Don't believe anything he says. Don't believe anything *anyone* says, from now on. It's the Festival of Lies and everything is back to front.' She stopped, then said, 'Oh, yes, and we have to talk in lies, too.'

'Even when we're talking to each other?' whispered Bonnie.

'Not when it's just us,' said Goldie. 'But when there are other people around I think we'd better. Unless we're touching an animal. Then we can tell the truth.'

The cat led the way into the tunnel, which was even darker than Goldie remembered. She gritted her teeth and felt her way along the slimy walls, with Bonnie clinging to her jacket and Toadspit bringing up the rear. The dripping sound was louder tonight, and she could hear water gurgling through underground cisterns somewhere nearby.

When she thought they had gone approximately halfway, she stopped and called out softly. 'Pounce? Mouse? Are you there?'

There was no answer, but Goldie thought she could hear someone breathing. 'Pounce?' she said. 'Is that you?'

'Nah,' said Pounce's rough voice. 'It's the bogey-man.'

A tinderbox scraped, and a yellow light sprang up. Directly in front of the three children, hanging in mid-air like a phantom, was a hairy snout, with long silver tusks and little, wicked, glinting eyes.

Bonnie squeaked with fright. Toadspit leaped forward to stand in front of her.

'I know that's not you, Pounce,' hissed Goldie.

There was a moment's silence, then Pounce moved the lantern so that Goldie could see his skinny arms. 'What do ya think this is, a boardin' 'ouse?' he said. He turned his back on them and began to walk up the tunnel.

Goldie hurried after him. 'I knew you'd be pleased to see us.'

'Yeah,' muttered Pounce. 'Whoopee.'

They turned the corner, and he lifted the blanket to one side. 'No one there, Mousie,' he said. 'Just ghoulies and gobblings.'

Mouse smiled when he saw Goldie, and the cat rubbed itself against him, purring. Toadspit and Bonnie eyed the two boys uncertainly, then Toadspit pushed his sister towards the fire and crouched next to her.

There was an old kettle perched on the edge of the fireplace. Mouse wedged it in among the coals, dug out two tin mugs and put a trickle of brown powder in each one.

Pounce leaned against the wall with his arms folded. 'You give 'em everythin' we got, Mousie,' he said sourly. 'They're welcome guests, they are. They can stay as long as they like.'

Mouse grinned. Goldie said, 'We'll be here for weeks, Pounce, you'll see. We'll be back tomorrow night, sure as anything. We're never going home if we can help it.'

Pounce shrugged. Mouse took the kettle off the fire and poured hot water onto the powder. The smell of chocolate filled the little room. He grimaced at Goldie as if to apologise for the fact that there were only two mugs, then gave one to Bonnie and the other to Toadspit. They wrinkled their noses at the steam and gulped the hot chocolate thankfully. The cat leaped up onto the stones beside them and closed its eyes, soaking in the warmth of the fire.

'It's the cat from the ship,' said Bonnie. 'I didn't realise.'

'You mean it's *not* the cat from the ship,' said Goldie.

'Oh,' said Bonnie. 'Yes. I mean, no. I mean—' She shook her head in confusion.

The cat yawned. Its wet spotted fur was plastered to its body, and for the first time Goldie saw the length of its legs, the enormous paws and the deceptive stillness.

Just like an idlecat! she thought. Then she laughed at herself, because idlecats were many times bigger than this and had been extinct for hundreds of years. And besides, if this was an idlecat, it would certainly have killed them all by now.

Still, there was something uncanny about the creature, and she was amazed that she had been bold enough to pick it up.

When Toadspit finished his hot chocolate, Mouse made another one for Goldie. Then he whistled. There was a rustling sound from the pram in the corner, and the mice peeled over the side like a breaking wave and scurried up onto the boy's shoulders. He crooned softly to them. Two of them trotted down his arm to his hand.

Bonnie leaned forward, wide-eyed. The mice sat up on their haunches and inspected her, their tiny noses twitching.

'They won't bite her, will they?' said Toadspit.

'Course they will,' said Pounce. 'They're man-eaters, they are. They dragged an old lady in 'ere earlier, and there's nothin' left of her now but false teeth and undies.'

Toadspit rolled his eyes. Bonnie laughed and stroked one of the mice with the tip of her finger.

Goldie wrapped her hands around the hot mug. 'They don't tell fortunes.'

'Can they tell ours?' asked Bonnie.

Mouse whistled again, and the mice raced back to the pram and returned with a dozen scraps of paper. The boy rejected them one by one, until there were only three left.

The first was a picture of a cat. The second said *too much water*. The third said *at the last minute, a lady of high birth*.

Bonnie's face fell. 'It doesn't— I mean, it *does* make sense.'

Mouse laughed. He picked up three of the mice and gave one to each of the children. Goldie closed her fingers around the small quivering body. 'Good,' she said. 'Now we can tell the truth.'

She stared at the bits of paper. 'The first one— It might mean the cat's coming with us when we leave here. Maybe that's important for some reason.'

The cat blinked slowly and leaned closer to the fire.

'The second one is probably the sea – perhaps that's how we're going home. It'd be much faster than going by road. And the third one— I think the third one must be the Protector.'

'High birth?' said Toadspit. 'That means a queen, or someone like that. Royalty.'

'But we haven't got a queen,' said Goldie. 'So it *must* be the Protector. Maybe she's trying to find us!'

Bonnie's eyes were worried. 'But what about the Festival? Didn't you say everything's a lie? Maybe the fortune's a lie too.'

'Is it?' said Goldie to Mouse. 'Do the fortunes lie during the Festival?'

The white-haired boy cuddled one of the mice against his cheek and shook his head.

Goldie felt a surge of relief. Even without one of the Big Lies, she had managed to get her friends away from Harrow. And now they had a fortune – a true fortune. A *good* fortune!

But they were not safe yet, she reminded herself. They would not be safe until they were far away from Spoke, and Harrow could no longer get his hands on them.

He's probably out there right now, searching for us.

And despite the warmth of the fire, she shivered at the thought of what would happen if he caught them.

Deep in the back rooms of the museum, Sinew and Broo were stalking the slommerkin. Sinew had not yet seen the creature. In fact, he had *never* seen one – they had been driven to extinction long before he was born. But he had heard about them. Heard how fast they were, how ferocious. Heard about their enormous bulk, and the way they liked to roll on their victims to soften them up for eating.

It would be a disaster if such a creature escaped into the city. And so the keeper and the brizzlehound had been on its trail for hours, following the smell that it left in its wake. Now at last they were closing in.

'It is in the next room.' Broo's hackles rose. 'We will trap it there and I will KILL it!'

'No,' whispered Sinew, inching towards the door that led to Old Mine Shafts. 'There will be no killing.'

'What else can you do with a slommerkin?' rumbled Broo. 'They are very stupid. All they think about is food.'

'It doesn't matter. This creature is probably the last of its kind, like you. We're going to try to drive it towards the Dirty Gate. Dan and Olga Ciavolga are up there waiting for us.'

Broo flattened his ears. 'Slommerkins cannot be driven like geese.'

'You're probably right, but we have to try nonetheless.' Sinew stifled a sneeze. 'Whew, it does stink, doesn't it!'

He pulled a kerchief out of his pocket and wrapped it around his face, covering his long nose. 'I hate to think of what must be happening to the children to bring something like this out of the woodwork. I keep hoping it'll go to sleep in a corner somewhere, and we'll know that everything's all right, that the children are safe.' He grimaced. 'But I don't think that's going to happen.'

'It does not smell sleepy.'

'No, it doesn't.' Sinew paused. 'Do you think it'll fight when it sees us, or will it keep running?'

'It will run. And *then* it will fight.'

Sinew unslung his harp. 'Well then, we'd best get on with it. Are you ready?'

The brizzlehound stiffened. His great shadow swooped up the walls, as black as a nightmare. His eyes glowed.

'I am RRRREADY!' he growled.

And he and Sinew leaped out of hiding and raced towards the slommerkin.

FLENSE

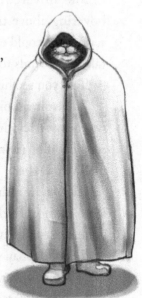

'**G**unna be a warm night,' muttered Pounce, poking at the fire. 'Don't reckon we'll need no more wood.'

He pushed past Toadspit and disappeared down the tunnel. As soon as he had gone, Toadspit turned to Goldie. 'So how do we get out of Spoke? And don't lie, it's just us.'

Goldie looked at the nest of quilts beside the fire, where Bonnie and Mouse were sound

Flense

asleep with the cat curled up between them. 'I'm not sure,' she whispered. 'I don't know who we can trust. The man who had you imprisoned—'

'Harrow?'

The cat's ear flicked as if it had been stung. 'Ssshhh!' said Goldie. 'He's got people everywhere.'

'Not *here*,' said Toadspit.

'Maybe not, but—' Goldie remembered the band-master's terrified face. *'You've signed my death warrant, and that of all my fellows!'*

She shivered. Harrow was like a black shadow hovering above the city. She wished— Oh, how she *wished* she could catch one of the Big Lies, and use it to take her friends to safety.

'Did you see him?' she whispered.

Toadspit shook his head. 'I heard Cord say that he was busy on another job. The woman in the green cloak seemed to be running things.'

'Who is she?'

'All I know is that her name's Flense. She stayed away from us most of the time, and when she was there she wore a mask. I never even heard her speak.'

'Did Cord say why they stole Bonnie?'

'No. Not a word.'

Goldie lowered her voice even more. '*I* found out something. Harrow's a murderer. He's killed at least a dozen people. And you know the bomb that destroyed the Fugleman's office? That was him! Or his men, at least.'

Toadspit stared at her. 'Are you *sure*?'

'N-No. But I think it's probably true.'

'Why would he bomb the Fugleman's office?'

'I don't know.'

Silence fell between them. Goldie chewed her knuckles, wondering how on earth they were going to get back home without being caught.

Presently Toadspit said, 'Look, we're going to have to trust *someone*.'

'Are we? The fortune said we're going home by sea. If we Concealed ourselves and stowed away on a ship—'

'You and I could do it easily enough, but what about Bonnie? If Harrow's— If *his* men caught her—'

He stopped, as the blanket that covered the tunnel was pushed to one side and Pounce entered, his arms piled high with fence palings.

'Don't worry 'bout me,' said Pounce. His mask glared at Goldie and Toadspit. 'These old things is light as a feather.'

He unloaded the palings into a corner, then sat down and poked at the fire. Toadspit leaned forward. 'Listen, Pounce. If we *didn't* want to go to Jewel—'

Goldie shook her head at him, but Toadspit ignored her. 'If we didn't want to go to Jewel, and we didn't want to go soon, *really* soon, what's the worst way to get there?'

Pounce jabbed at the fire. 'This your job?' he said to Goldie. 'The one that don't pay?'

Goldie didn't answer. She didn't trust Pounce, and wished that Toadspit hadn't asked him for help. But it was too late to do anything about it now.

'Anyone else involved?' said Pounce. 'Like, anyone who might want to *stop* ya gettin' to Jewel?'

'No,' said Toadspit, meaning yes.

'Yes,' said Goldie, meaning no.

'Make up yer minds,' sniggered Pounce. 'Someone chasin' yez, or not?'

Goldie leaned forward fiercely. 'Stick your nose into our business as much as you like, Pounce. Can you help us, or can't you?'

'All right, all right,' said the boy, holding his hands up. 'I reckon— I reckon maybe I can't.' He hesitated. 'Any money in it?'

Goldie shook her head. 'Definitely not. Not if we get home safely.'

'Mm,' said Pounce. 'That's nasty. Maybe I won't go and talk to someone.' He stood up and slouched towards the curtain.

'Pounce,' said Goldie.

The boy turned around. 'What?'

'Don't keep this to yourself. Tell everyone. *Every-*one.'

Pounce saluted mockingly. His eyes glittered behind the mask – and he was gone.

When Goldie woke up some hours later, the lantern was guttering and Pounce was leaning over her.

'I didn't find a ship,' he whispered, sounding pleased with himself. 'Captain's not a mate of mine. Ain't leavin' in an hour. Ain't goin' straight to Jewel.'

Goldie scrambled to her feet. 'Will you take us to him?'

Pounce snorted. 'Course I will. *I* ain't got nothin' better to do than take foreign snotties on a guided tour of the city.'

'How are we going to find him then?'

'A map'd be no use.' Pounce turned away, then swung back again. Something clinked in his britches pocket. 'You make lots of noise while yer gettin' ready,' he hissed. 'Mousie ain't tired, don't need 'is beauty sleep. You make as much noise as ya like.'

While Goldie tiptoed around the little room, waking Toadspit and Bonnie, Pounce stuck another stub of candle in the lantern and drew a map on the wall of the tunnel in charcoal. When he had finished, the three children from Jewel crowded around him.

Pounce stabbed at the bottom of the map with a blackened finger. 'We ain't 'ere,' he said. He stabbed again. 'And the wharf ain't 'ere.'

Goldie bent closer and saw five stick figures. Further up was a picture of what might have been a boat.

'This,' continued Pounce, tapping a squarish blotch near the wharf, 'ain't a deserted stableyard. Me mate won't be waitin' for yez there.'

His finger went back to the beginning. 'Now, 'ow do yez get to the stables from 'ere? It's real 'ard. First, don't go up this street. Then—'

His hand moved up the map. His britches pocket clinked.

Clink. Clink clink clink . . .

Goldie would have liked to have said goodbye to Mouse, but he was still asleep and, whenever she looked in his direction, Pounce's mask glared at her. So she whispered her thanks and farewells to the pram instead, and hoped that somehow the mice would understand and pass her message onto their boy.

It was hard to leave the warmth of the little room. But at least they were not alone – the cat went with them, just as the fortune had promised. Goldie was glad. Harrow and his men were still out there somewhere, and she wanted her allies around her.

We'll have Morg, too, she thought.

But when they reached the mouth of the tunnel, there was no sign of the slaughterbird.

Toadspit bit his lip. 'We should wait for her. She won't be far away.'

'We can't afford the time,' said Goldie. 'Don't worry; she'll catch up with us. If she found us once, she can find us again.'

'Are you lying?' said Bonnie.

Goldie smiled. 'No, it's just us now. We don't have to lie.'

'What do you reckon the time is?' said Toadspit.

'I don't know,' said Goldie. 'Two o'clock in the morning? Half past?'

With the cat trotting beside them, they set out along the dark streets, following the directions they had memorised from Pounce's map. The rain had stopped, but streams sprouted in all directions, as if the earth was so full of water that it was leaking.

There weren't many people around, and the only sound of the Festival was the occasional distant popping of thunderflashes. As the children approached the wharf, even that died away.

The stableyard was halfway along a row of derelict houses. It had a high stone wall around it and only one gateway. There was no light showing.

The children and the cat stopped several houses away. 'I thought Pounce's friend would be here by now,' whispered Goldie. She looked at the gate uneasily. In the back of her mind the little voice whispered, *Beware*.

'He's probably inside, waiting for us,' said Bonnie. 'Let's go in. I'm freezing.'

Toadspit shook his head. 'If he's here, why isn't he showing a light? I don't like it. That yard's a good place for a trap.'

'I'm going to have a closer look,' said Goldie. 'You two wait here.'

Toadspit nodded. 'Be careful.'

With the cat trotting beside her, Goldie circled around the block so that she could come at the stableyard from behind. Her feeling of unease was growing, and she pressed her mask firmly in place and wished that she had thought to bring masks for her friends. But it was too late now. Silently, she climbed the stone wall, slid down into the yard and opened her senses to the night.

The moon was covered by cloud, and her eyes told her very little. She could see the dark bulk of the deserted stalls and something that might have been an old cart. Nothing else.

Beside her, the cat's tail switched back and forth.

Goldie's nose told her that the yard hadn't been used by humans for years. It stank of wet feathers and fur. Of tiny battles. Of winter hunger, and the sudden spurt of hot blood.

Her ears told her . . . nothing at all.

Her skin prickled. A place that smelled like this should be full of small sounds. The patter of paws. The sleepy shuffle of birds. The squeal of unexpected death.

Instead, an unnatural stillness hung over the stable-yard, as if the creatures that normally lived here were holding their breath, waiting for some greater predator to leave.

What were they afraid of, she wondered. Her? The cat? Or . . .

'There's someone else here, isn't there?' she whispered to the cat. 'Where are they? Can you show me?'

The cat bumped against her, then stalked away across the yard. Goldie followed, putting her feet down heel-to-silent-toe, the way she had learned in the museum. The first row of horse stalls loomed up, then the second.

Goldie crept along the back of them, wondering where the cat was taking her.

Then she saw it – the faintest of lights shining through a grating.

She touched the back of the stall with her fingertips and felt a vibration, as if someone had grown tired of standing still and was shifting from one foot to the other. She stood on tiptoe and peeped through the grating.

The first thing she saw was a lantern. It hung from the ceiling of the stall, its light almost totally hidden by iron shutters. In the single faint beam that remained, Goldie could just make out a shadowy figure.

A *familiar* figure wearing a green cloak and a cat mask.

It was Flense.

Goldie could have cried with disappointment. All her hopes for a quick journey home crashed to the ground. There was no ship leaving for Jewel. There was no safe passage. Pounce had betrayed them.

The woman moved her feet again. 'Come on,' she whispered. 'Where are you, brats? Come on.'

When Goldie heard that voice, her wrist began to burn as if there was a silver cuff rubbing against it. Her skin crawled.

No, she thought. *No, it's not possible . . .*

'By the Black Ox!' muttered the woman. 'Where *are*

they?' She pushed her mask up onto her forehead and rubbed her eyes. Her cloak swirled. The narrow beam of the lantern fell across her face.

Goldie blinked. The stableyard swam around her, as if the world had tipped on its axis. The cat mask winked malevolently.

A cat . . .

But it was not the memory of the fortune that made Goldie tremble. Nor was it Pounce's treachery. She crept away from the stalls, her whole body cold with shock. The cat leaped over the wall ahead of her, and she followed it, stumbling around the block and down the deserted street to where her friends were waiting.

She could feel Toadspit's eyes on her as she approached. 'It's a trap, isn't it,' he whispered.

Goldie nodded. Swallowed. Touched her mask. Could hardly believe what she had seen.

'What?' whispered Toadspit. 'Tell me.'

'The woman in the green cloak. Flense. The one who's running things for Harrow. She's— She's—'

'Ffffoul!' spat the cat, whipping its tail from side to side.

'She's—'

'*Tell* me!'

Goldie took a shaky breath. 'She's *Blessed Guardian Hope*!'

TRAPPED

Toadspit and Bonnie stared at Goldie in horror. Blessed Guardian Hope, the woman who had tried to sell Goldie into slavery! The woman who, along with the Fugleman, had nearly destroyed Jewel.

'But she's dead!' said Bonnie. 'She drowned six months ago, her and the Fugleman.'

Mouse

'Ssshhh! No one ever found their bodies.'

'No, but—'

'We have to get away from here,' said Goldie. 'She'll realise something's wrong soon and come looking for us.'

'Where can we go?' said Bonnie.

Toadspit scowled. 'Back to the sewers. I'm going to wring Pounce's neck.'

'We could still try the wharves,' said Goldie. 'Maybe there really are ships leaving for Jewel. Maybe that bit was true.'

'How will we know if they're safe?' said Bonnie.

Goldie and Toadspit looked at each other. 'We won't,' said Toadspit. 'Not if Harrow's *really* got people all over the place.'

'We'll have to go by land,' said Goldie. 'It'll take a lot longer—'

'You want us to *walk*?' Bonnie's voice rose in a squeal of disbelief. 'All the way to *Jewel*?'

'Sssshhhh!' hissed Toadspit and Goldie together.

But it was too late. In the still of the night, Bonnie's voice rang out like a signal. There was a shout from inside the stableyard – and feet pounded out the gate towards them.

The children turned and ran. Back past the empty houses with their gaping windows. Around a corner.

Across a gushing stream – a leap almost too much for Bonnie. Past a knacker's yard, past a row of boarded-up shops, with the cat galloping beside them, its tail high, its ears flat against its skull.

As they ran, a single question rattled in Goldie's head like a pebble in a tin. *What was Guardian Hope doing here?*

Most of the streetlamps in this part of town were broken, and there were places where it was so dark that Goldie could barely see five steps in front of her. Once she nearly ran straight into a wall. *Watch out!* cried the little voice, and she swerved just in time, with a cry of warning to the others.

They ran down street after street. They ducked around corners and dived through alleyways. But try as they would, they could not lose their pursuers. Before long, Goldie's heart felt as if it might explode in her chest.

She saw a narrow lane between two buildings. The cat leaped into it, and the three children followed. Behind them, someone howled with excitement, like a dog that has sighted a hare.

At the end of the lane, Goldie looked around wildly. 'Which way?' she said to the cat.

In the wall beside her, a battered tin door swung open. A small hand beckoned urgently.

'Mouse!'

Toadspit grabbed Goldie's arm. 'No. We can't trust him.'

'They didn't go this way, Cord,' shouted a voice from the mouth of the lane. 'I'm not right on their tail. Woohoo!'

Goldie wrenched her arm out of Toadspit's grasp and leaped for the doorway, with Bonnie right behind her. Toadspit hesitated, then jumped after them.

They raced through the derelict rooms and down a flight of stone stairs to a small damp cellar. In front of them was the entrance to a tunnel with a barred gate across it. Goldie could hear running water.

'Another – old sewer?' gasped Toadspit.

Mouse nodded.

'Is there a way – out – the other end? No lies!'

The little boy nodded again.

The gate was rusted into position, but there was a gap that Bonnie and Mouse could slip through easily. It was more of a struggle for the two older children. Goldie heard Smudge's heavy feet pounding down the stairs towards them.

'Quick,' she said, and she squeezed through the gate after Toadspit.

The tunnel was pitch black and narrow. The children felt their way down it, sliding their hands over the brick walls and brushing spider webs from their faces. They had not gone more than ten paces when the tunnel turned a corner. They hurried around it – and ran straight into a rockfall.

Mouse yelped. Toadspit and Bonnie shouted with the shock of it. Goldie fumbled at the pile of rocks and broken bricks, trying to find a way past them. But they filled the tunnel from top to bottom. There was no escape.

She leaned against the wall, trying to catch her breath. Toadspit turned on Mouse. 'It's a trap,' he snarled. 'You brought us here on purpose.'

Somewhere near Goldie's feet, the cat hissed a warning.

'Listen,' whispered Bonnie. 'It's Smudge. He's trying to get through the gate!'

Smudge grunted and swore, but the gap was too small and the gate would not open wider to let him past. After a minute or two he gave up. Goldie heard him shout, 'Hey, Cord. I think I ain't got 'em trapped.'

There was an answering shout from Cord. 'How many?'

'I didn't see four.'

Cord's feet thumped down the stairs, and the glow of a lantern seeped into the tunnel. 'Ha! They don't keep multiplyin'.'

'Where's Flense got to?' said Smudge. 'Don't tell her that it were me who caught 'em!'

Bonnie was shivering. Goldie put her arms around the younger girl. 'Don't worry, Princess Frisia,' she whispered, 'Morg'll find us. She'll get into the building somehow. She'll chase them away.'

Toadspit grunted. 'They'll be expecting her this time.'

'We're not going to give up, are we?' said Bonnie.

'No,' whispered Goldie. 'Harrow's far too dangerous.'

Mouse nodded and drew his finger across his throat in a gesture that made her skin crawl.

'Goldie, are you *sure* it was Guardian Hope you saw?' whispered Toadspit. 'It doesn't make sense. What would she be doing here? Why would she be working for someone like Harrow?'

'I don't know—' Goldie stopped. All the things she had seen and heard over the last few days tumbled through her head, making unexpected patterns . . .

She let go of Bonnie. 'The bomb!'

'What bomb?' whispered Bonnie. 'You mean the one in the Fugleman's office?'

'Yes. That was Harrow. At least, someone told me it was. But why would he do such a thing?' The patterns shifted. The bits clicked into place like pins in a padlock. '*Who gained from it?*'

THE KEEPERS | CITY OF LIES

'No one,' said Toadspit.

Goldie shook her head. 'Don't you remember? Before the bombing, there was a rumour that the Protector was going to halve the number of Blessed Guardians. And everyone was really pleased. But *after* the bombing, they were so frightened that they wanted *more* Guardians, not fewer. They almost doubled their numbers overnight.'

'But—' said Toadspit.

'Listen,' breathed Goldie. '*Guardian Hope* is Flense. I saw her! So who's Harrow? Who would she work for? Who is the *only* person Guardian Hope would work for?'

For a moment there was complete silence except for the sound of running water. Then Toadspit said, in a shocked voice, 'It's— It's the Fugleman! It must be. He's still alive. He had Bonnie stolen. *He bombed his own office!*'

At the entrance to the tunnel, someone cleared their throat. Iron shutters scraped and lantern light splashed across the children's faces.

The blood froze in Goldie's veins.

'Well well,' said Guardian Hope. 'Have you noticed, Cord, how these old sewers magnify the slightest whisper? If a person happened to be listening, a person could hear the most *interesting* things.'

The Fugleman was having trouble with all this humility. It rubbed against his skin like sacking. He loathed it.

He loathed the dungeons too. And so, last night, he had set out to persuade his guards to let him sleep in the office for a change. He had smiled his charming smile, and twisted the truth this way and that like toffee. Before five minutes had passed, the guards were smiling back at him. Before ten minutes, they thought the whole sleeping-in-the-office thing was their idea.

It was wonderfully easy when he put his mind to it.

As a result, he was dozing in a comfortable chair when the runner from the semaphore station arrived. He heard his guards jerk upright. He raised his own head more slowly.

'Your Honour,' said the runner. 'An urgent message has come through.' She thrust an envelope into his hand.

The message was coded, of course, like all the others he had received. It was a simple code, one that he had worked out with Guardian Hope several weeks ago.

'*Think we have found children*' meant '*Have brats under lock and key*'.

'*Closing in on villains*' meant '*All goes according to plan, no one suspects us*'.

They had allowed for things to go wrong. But he had never seriously expected to see the message that now lay before him.

'Children not sighted since last report. Believe they are still alive, but extremely ill. Please advise.'

His gorge rose, so that he felt as if he might vomit. He forced himself to be still.

'Are you *sure* of this wording?' he asked the young woman. 'I know the semaphore is difficult at night. Perhaps not all of the lamps were lit.'

'They ran the check code, Your Honour, just to be sure. All the lamps are working.'

'Is there a problem?' said one of the guards, leaning over to peer at the bit of paper.

'Read for yourself,' said the Fugleman, keeping his face blank only by an enormous effort. A terrible fury was growing inside him and he wanted to leap out of his chair and scream at the man.

Of course there's a problem, you moron! The brats escaped! They've been recaptured, but somehow they have discovered the truth. The WHOLE truth!

The guard read the message out loud. 'Extremely ill? I don't like the sound of that.'

'Neither do I. But we must— We must not give up,' muttered the Fugleman. He grabbed a pen and paper and began to scratch out a coded reply, his hand pushing so hard on the pen that the nib broke.

He took a new one and started again. 'Here,' he said, 'I'll read it aloud as I write.' He cleared his throat. 'Use all available resources. Rescue . . . them . . . tonight. Repeat . . . tonight. Repeat . . . rescue.'

He blotted the ink, put the message in an envelope and gave it to the runner. She ducked her head and mumbled, 'I just wanted to say, Your Honour, we all appreciate your efforts to save the children.' Then she dashed out the door.

As the sound of her footsteps receded, the Fugleman leaned back in his chair. 'Now,' he said, 'it is up to my informants – and the will of the Seven Gods.'

The guards flicked their fingers. 'It was good, Your Honour,' said the youngest one, 'the way you repeated bits of it. That'll get them moving.'

'I certainly hope so,' murmured the Fugleman.

In his mind, he was replaying the message he had sent. '*Use all available resources.*'

That was the important part, the bit that would set his back-up plan in motion. He was glad now that he had decided to have a back-up. Of course, it would have been so much more *satisfying* to do the whole thing by his own wits, and the Southern Archipelago mercenaries were appallingly expensive. But they were about to prove their worth. With luck he would be free within a day or so, and the city of Jewel would be under his heel at last.

The second part of the message was really just an afterthought. But it was important to tie up loose ends. And the children were a *very* loose end.

He chuckled silently to himself, his rage entirely gone. The youngest guard would be surprised if he knew what the *real* message was. The one that Hope would act on.

'*Kill them tonight. Repeat – tonight. Repeat – kill them.*'

TOO MUCH WATER

The light from Cord's lantern seeped into the tunnel like a false dawn. Mouse's face was white with misery. His little pets huddled on his shoulders, pressing themselves against his bare neck as if they were trying to warm him. The sound of running water was growing louder.

'I think Morg's forgotten about us,' said Bonnie. She was shivering. They all were, except for the cat, which was crouched on a ledge three-quarters of the way up the tunnel wall, cleaning its paws.

Toadspit

Goldie touched Mouse's arm. 'Did Pounce send you?'

'Yeah,' growled Toadspit. 'Sent him to trap us.'

Mouse shook his head. He mimed waking up and finding that they had gone. He pretended to be Pounce, a *gleeful* Pounce, counting out a pile of coins from his britches pocket – more coins than Mouse had ever seen. He mimed himself discovering the map on the wall, and running desperately down to the deserted stableyard to warn them, only to find that the trap had been sprung.

He touched the rockfall, and showed them how recent it was – how it must have happened in the last day or so.

Toadspit grunted.

'*I* believe you,' said Bonnie, glaring at her brother.

'Does Pounce know you came after us?' said Goldie.

Mouse shook his head.

'I don't understand why—' began Bonnie.

'Sshh!' said Toadspit.

Goldie heard sharp footsteps on the stairs, and saw the light of a second lantern brighten the mouth of the tunnel. She quickly adjusted her mask. Guardian Hope had been gone for an hour or more, but now she was back.

'Hey, Flense,' said Smudge. 'The snotties have

disappeared, look. Did ya tell Harrow it weren't me who caught 'em?'

'Stop your stupid lies, idiot,' snapped Guardian Hope. 'The Festival is an Abomination in the eyes of the Seven Gods. *I* may wear a mask for my own *holy* purposes, but that is all. You will speak straight, both of you. Do you understand?'

'No. Er. Um. Yep,' mumbled Smudge.

'And you, Cord?'

'It's no skin off my nose,' said Cord.

'Any sign of that bird while I was gone?'

'Yeah. I mean, nah,' said Cord. 'But if it comes, we're ready for it.'

'Good,' said Guardian Hope. She tugged at the gate. 'Are you sure this thing won't open any further?'

'Won't budge,' said Cord. 'And we can't get through that gap.'

'Mm. That makes it interesting . . .' Guardian Hope raised her lantern so that the light splashed across the children. 'Why are there so many of them? There are only supposed to be two. Who are the others?'

'See that little snotty with white 'air?' said Cord. "E tells fortunes in the Spice Market. I dunno 'oo the one with the mask is, but 'e 'elped 'em escape last night.'

'Who are you, boy?' called Guardian Hope.

Goldie said nothing. A drip of water ran down the back of her neck.

'Well, whoever you are,' said Guardian Hope, 'you're going to be sorry you got mixed up in this.'

'What are you going to do with us?' called Toadspit, wrapping his arms around his sister.

'Well now, we *were* going to send you back home. And what a joyous occasion that would've been.' Guardian Hope laughed sourly. 'The lost children back in the arms of their frantic parents. Oh, there would have been dancing in the streets. There's nothing the citizens of Jewel care for so much as their brats.'

'What's the use of stealing us and then taking us home again?' Bonnie peered out from underneath Toadspit's arm. 'That's stupid.'

'*Stupid?*' snapped Guardian Hope. 'It was a *beautiful* plan! His Honour the Fugleman worked it out so carefully.'

'I don't understand,' said Toadspit, shivering.

'Of course you don't. That's because the *real* game is being played out in Jewel. You're just a tool.'

Guardian Hope's voice echoed up and down the tunnel. 'A tool . . . a tool . . . a tool . . .' Goldie hardly noticed. Her mind was stuck on those eight terrible words. '*We WERE going to send you back home.*'

She put her hand over her mouth to stop herself

crying out. If she hadn't rescued Bonnie and Toadspit, they would have been safe! They might even have been on their way home already!

But Hope *couldn't* let them go now. They knew too much. So what would she do? Keep them locked up? Sell them to one of the slavers who roamed the southern seas?

'You see,' continued Guardian Hope, 'His Honour is in Jewel at this very moment. He gave himself up, asked to be punished for his crimes. Poor shattered creature.'

She sniggered. '*He* was the one who traced you to Spoke, you know, after you were "stolen". If it wasn't for him you would have been lost forever. Now tell me, do you think the citizens of Jewel would let the Protector imprison the man who got their lost children back? No, of course not. They'd forgive him. They'd want him in his old job, keeping their brats safe. Because the Protector couldn't keep them safe, could she? Why, there have been all *sorts* of incidents in the last few weeks. A broken leg. A near-drowning. And if this missing children business didn't do the trick, I expect we would have had a *proper* drowning soon. Perhaps even a murder.'

Her voice rose angrily. 'All the changes the Protector has made, and look what happens. Get rid of her, I say. Bring back the Fugleman! Bring back the Blessed Guardians—'

She stopped and cleared her throat. 'But now, because of your oh-so-clever guesswork, His Honour will be forced to use his back-up plan instead. An army of mercenaries from the Southern Archipelago. How Jewel will tremble!'

She laughed. 'As for you children, the Fugleman has sent new orders. It seems that you're not going home to your loving parents after all.'

Goldie's legs began to shake. Slavers. It must be the slavers.

In the back of her mind, the little voice whispered, *Squeeze around the corner where she can't see you.*

'Shut up,' said Goldie under her breath. 'I should never have listened to you in the first place! I should have left Bonnie and Toadspit where they were!'

Squeeze around the corner—

'Shut up. Shut up shut up shut up!'

Squeeze around—

'SHUT UP!'

The sudden silence in the back of her mind was a shock. But a *good* one, she told herself. She had trusted the little voice, and it had betrayed her. It had betrayed all of them.

She found herself thinking about Ma and Pa, and how they had suffered because of her. A spasm of self-loathing shot through her.

On the stairs outside the tunnel, Smudge seemed to be arguing with Guardian Hope and Cord. 'What, all of 'em?' he said, in a puzzled voice. 'Even the snotty with the mice? 'E told my fortune once. I don't reckon we should—'

'Yer not paid to reckon,' interrupted Cord. 'You just keep yer trap shut and do what yer told. If Harrow wants 'em shot, then we shoot 'em.'

Shoot us? The air in Goldie's lungs turned to ice. Beside her, Bonnie, Toadspit and Mouse gasped with shock.

'I didn't say *shoot* them, you fool,' snapped Guardian Hope. 'I said *drown* them.'

'What's the difference? They're just as dead.'

'If we shoot them, it's murder. And it will raise far too many questions when their bodies are found. But if they drown, it's just – an unfortunate accident.'

'How we gunna drown 'em if we can't get at 'em?' said Cord.

'That's the beauty of it.' Guardian Hope sat down on the stairs and raised her voice so that Goldie could hear every awful word. 'There was a time when the city used these old sewers to drown pirates. A bit of rain and a high tide, and the water comes pouring in. It fills the whole cellar. Well, we've had the rain, and high tide is just after sunrise. All we have to do is wait here and make sure they don't escape.'

'T-Too much water!' whispered Bonnie.

Goldie's legs were shaking more than ever. She tried to control them and couldn't. This was her fault. This was all her fault.

'But I don't—' said Smudge.

'Quiet!' Cord's voice was urgent. 'I 'eard somethin' up near the roof. I think it's the bird.'

Toadspit shuddered, as if he was trying to fight his way out of a nightmare. He grabbed Goldie's hand. His fingers signed an urgent message against her skin. *This our best chance. Come on.*

Goldie stared at him. She felt as if a thick fog was pressing in on her from all sides. Or perhaps it was a chain, an invisible chain, wrapping its links so tightly around her that she could not move.

Her friends were going to die. And it was her fault.

Come on! signed Toadspit.

Still Goldie could not move. Toadspit stared at her, puzzled, then turned and threw himself down the tunnel, crying, 'Morg! Morg! We're *here!*'

There was a great flapping of wings outside the bars. One of the lanterns fell over, and Smudge shouted in fright. Guardian Hope screamed, 'Get it! Shoot it! Catch it in the net!'

Goldie heard a pistol shot. 'Aaaark!' screeched Morg, and fell to the ground with a thump.

Cord whooped with delight. 'I winged it. Quick, chuck the net over it, Smudge.'

'What've you done to her?' cried Toadspit. 'Morg, are you all right?'

Morg screeched again – with fury this time.

'Ooh, it don't like bein' trapped,' said Cord. 'Just as well the net's nice and strong. Look at that nasty old beak.' He chortled. 'Nearly took your eye out, Smudge.'

'It's a demon bird,' muttered Smudge. 'Put a bullet through its 'ead.'

'No!' cried Toadspit. He fumbled on the floor of the tunnel, picked up a large stone and threw it through the bars.

'Ow!' said Cord. 'You little—'

'Remember what I said, Cord!' But Guardian Hope's warning came too late.

A second pistol shot echoed up and down the tunnel. Something *clanged* against the bars – and Toadspit collapsed in a heap.

The slommerkin made its stand in Forgotten Dreams. It had been running for hour upon hour, but now it turned, as if something had stung it, and came at Sinew

197

in a rush. Its tusks dripped foulness. Its monstrous bulk swelled with rage.

The long chase had exhausted Sinew and, for the briefest of moments, he stood rooted to the spot. Then he dived to one side, fingers instinctively plucking at his harp strings. The notes of the First Song spun out around him.

It was a ridiculously feeble weapon for the circumstances, he knew that. Without Broo, he would have been dead within seconds. The brizzlehound threw himself into the path of the charging slommerkin, and the two of them disappeared in a whirl of teeth and tusks.

The sound of their battle was appalling, and it was almost impossible to see what was happening. At first Sinew thought Broo had the upper hand. He saw the brizzlehound fasten his great teeth into the slommerkin's neck and heard a squeal of pain. But Forgotten Dreams was a room where things slipped away before you could grasp them, and the next thing he saw was the slommerkin gripping *Broo's* neck, as if it had been that way all along. Then that too was gone.

He closed his eyes, knowing he could not trust them, and bent his head to his harp. His fingers ripped at the strings, trying to slide the notes of the First Song in between those awful tusks to wherever the slommerkin kept its brain.

He did not know how long he played. Once, he opened his eyes and noticed, with surprise, that his fingers were bleeding. He caught a glimpse of the slommerkin and Broo, tearing at each other's blood-soaked bodies. He thought of Goldie and Toadspit and Bonnie, and knew that, wherever they were, they too must be fighting for their lives.

He closed his eyes again and played more furiously than ever.

AT THE LAST MINUTE, A LADY OF HIGH BIRTH

Goldie No One

Goldie's feet were numb with cold and she was shivering uncontrollably. The water, pouring into the tunnel from a dozen small pipes, had already reached her knees. She thought that sunrise must be very close.

Her fault. It was all her fault . . .

Toadspit was alive but unconscious. In the confusion after the shooting, the other children had managed to drag him back up the tunnel to the corner. Goldie had pressed a clump of spider webs against the side of his head until the bullet wound stopped bleeding, then made a bandage from the sleeve of Bonnie's blouse.

Now she held him more-or-less upright, propped against the wall, with Mouse and Bonnie clinging to the bricks beside him. The cat crouched on the ledge, its eyes huge and dark, its tattered ears flat against its skull. Goldie wondered if it could swim. Maybe it would be able to save itself, once she and her friends were dead.

Perhaps the mice would swim away too, when they could no longer help their boy. But for now they fussed quietly over him, like a dozen tiny mothers, rubbing their whiskers against his face and cleaning whichever parts of him they could reach.

Goldie had never in her life felt so heartsick. If it wasn't for her, Toadspit and Bonnie would be on their way home, and Mouse would still be telling fortunes in the Spice Market. But now . . .

Bonnie was trying hard not to cry. Goldie put her arm around the younger girl. 'I'm s-sorry,' she said. The shivering made her voice waver. She felt terribly tired. Perhaps in a little while she would lie down and go to sleep.

'Wh-what for?' said Bonnie.

'If I'd l-left you there, none of this would've h-happened. It's m-my fault.'

Mouse tapped her on the arm, and pointed miserably at his own small chest, then at the rock pile. *My* fault, he seemed to say.

Bonnie screwed up her nose. 'Don't be s-stupid,' she said through chattering teeth. 'You're both s-stupid.'

'But it *is* my f-fault—' began Goldie.

'In that c-case,' said Bonnie, 'it's *m-m-my* fault too. I'm the one who made too much noise outside the s-s-stables. If I hadn't d-done that we probably would have g-got away.'

Her voice rose. 'But I'm *n-not* the one who shot my b-b-brother. I'm *n-not* the one who's trying to d-drown us. And neither are you.' She was shouting now, her high voice bouncing off the tunnel walls. 'It's *their* fault.' She pointed furiously towards the gate. 'I *h-h-hate* them! And when we g-get out of here I'm going to t-teach them a lesson!'

There was a laugh from the stairs outside. The water crept upwards, as cold and remorseless as their captors' hearts. Goldie whispered, 'Bonnie, I— I don't think we *w-will* get out of—'

'Don't say that. We *w-will*. You'll think of something.' Tears poured down the younger girl's face. 'If my b-brother was awake,' she said fiercely, '*he'd* get us out. But he's not, so you'll d-do it instead. I *know* you will.' She glared at Mouse as if he had argued with her. 'You just w-wait and see!'

Goldie could not speak. Mouse was staring at her with desperate hope in his eyes. Even the cat and the white mice were watching her, as if they expected her to come up with a miracle.

I don't know any miracles, she thought.

But at the same time, something stirred inside her.

The Festival.

The Wildness.

The Big Lies . . .

A Big Lie might save them – *if* she could summon one. *If* they hadn't all been used up already.

With an enormous effort, Goldie forced her poor sluggish mind to cry out for help. 'Come to me,' she called silently. 'I need you. I *need* you!'

She tried to imagine the Wildness welling up beneath her, and the air fizzing around her, the way it had fizzed around the dancing girls.

She tried so hard.

And then she tried again.

And again.

She could feel herself sinking back into despair. 'There must be some way of summoning a Big Lie,' she whispered. 'Think! *Think!*'

But the cold water was up to her waist now, and it

gripped her like the hand of death. All she wanted to do was lie down and sleep.

Would that be such a bad thing?

No . . .

She was on the brink of giving up when, deep in the back of her mind, so far away that she could barely hear it, a little voice whispered, *Sing.*

'W-What?' mumbled Goldie.

Sing!

'S-s-sing *what*?'

But all the voice would say was *Sing* . . .

Goldie ransacked her numb brain for songs. But they had gone, along with the warmth of her body. The only one she could remember was the scrap of nonsense that she had heard on the streets of Spoke.

Not knowing what else to do, she began to mumble, *'And her – ch-children – were h-hairy – and t-terribly scary . . .'*

Even before the words died away, she knew it was useless. It would take a *big* song to get them out of here. A song that could shift a rock pile, or change the minds of heartless killers.

She closed her eyes and, like a distant echo, heard the *thrum* of a harp string. As if, hundreds of miles away, Sinew was playing the First Song. Playing for his life and the lives of others. Playing on and on and never giving up.

The First Song. Of course! How could she have forgotten? It was the song that every other song in the world had grown out of. Goldie had no idea what it might do if she sang it in Spoke. But she knew without a doubt that it would do *something* . . .

The rising tide was up to her armpits now. She still had hold of Toadspit, though she could not feel her hands. Mouse and Bonnie were struggling to keep their heads above water.

It would have been the easiest thing in the world to let go and slip beneath the surface. Nevertheless, Goldie opened her mouth and began to croak out the strange sliding notes of the First Song. *'Ho oh oh-oh. Mm mm oh oh oh-oh oh.'*

Her throat felt as if it belonged to someone else. She forced herself to keep going. *'Ho oh oh-oh. Mm mm oh oh.'*

For an unbearably long time, nothing happened. Then, all at once, the air around her flickered like a candle flame. Toadspit groaned.

'Mm mm oh,' croaked Goldie. *'Mm mm oh oh oh-oh oh.'*

The flickering feeling came again. As if— As if *something* was taking an interest in her. She sang louder. *'Ho oh oh-oh. Ho oh oh-oh. Mm mm oh oh oh-oh oh.'*

'What are you doing in there?' shouted Guardian Hope, who had climbed to a higher stair to avoid the rising water. 'What have you got to sing about?'

Goldie didn't reply. An unexpected warmth was surging through her body, giving her strength. She wrapped her arms as best she could around Toadspit and the other children, and kept singing. *'Ho oh oh-oh. Mm mm oh oh oh-oh oh.'*

The cat lifted its sodden ears and yowled along with her, *'Rrow rrow rrow-rrow. Prr prr rrow rrow rrow rrow-rrow.'* The white mice squeaked the same odd notes.

Toadspit, still deeply unconscious, mumbled, *'Mm mm oh oh oh-oh oh.'*

And then it happened. The air on every side began to swirl and fizz. Goldie's song twisted around her head as if she stood in the middle of a giant whirlpool.

Mouse's eyes were nearly popping out of his skull. 'W-What is it?' hissed Bonnie. 'What's happening?'

Goldie didn't reply. She was waiting for the right question. And racking her brain for the right answer . . .

Guardian Hope splashed down into the water and pressed her face to the bars. 'What are you doing?' she shouted again.

Cord's face appeared beside her. 'It's that other snotty,' he said. 'The one with the mask.'

'Here, you,' shouted Guardian Hope. 'Why are you singing?'

206

The water lapped at Goldie's collarbone. The air swirled around her, full of power and promise. *'Ho oh oh-oh,'* she sang. *'Mm mm oh oh oh-oh oh.'*

'Boy?' shouted Guardian Hope. 'Why are you singing? What do you think you are doing?' Her voice cracked with frustration. 'What's all this got to do with you anyway? *Who are you?*'

At last! The right question! But what was the right answer? It had to be something that got them *all* out of danger. Not just Goldie.

She knew that the swirling feeling wouldn't last for long. Already it was slightly weaker, as if it had given her a chance – and now it was moving on to someone else.

WHAT WAS THE RIGHT ANSWER?

In the back of her mind, the little voice whispered, *At the last minute, a lady of high birth.*

'What?' cried Goldie.

She could feel the whirlpool drawing away from her. She stared wildly around, searching for inspiration. Her eyes fell on Mouse, the cat, Toadspit, Bonnie—

Bonnie with her bow, wanting to be a champion archer! Bonnie on board the *Piglet*, giving Smudge the name of a long-dead warrior princess!

'Did you hear me, boy?' shouted Guardian Hope. '*Who are you?*'

As the whirlpool swirled one last time around her, Goldie drew herself up. 'I am Princess Frisia of Merne,' she cried. 'And everyone here is part of my court!'

And suddenly, the whole world changed . . .

SOMETHING HAS HAPPENED TO THE CHILDREN...

The slommerkin stopped its attack so abruptly that Sinew was taken by surprise. His fingers paused on the harp strings. Was this another illusion from Forgotten Dreams, or was it something else?

'Sinew,' growled Broo, backing slowly away from his opponent. 'Do not STOP!'

'Sorry,' said Sinew, and he plucked at the strings again.

The Slommerkin

The slommerkin shook its massive head, as if the notes of the First Song had at last wormed their way into its mind, and it could not escape them.

Sinew's fingers felt as if they were on fire, but he was in better shape than Broo. The brizzlehound was covered in blood and there was a deep gash down his shoulder and around his belly.

The slommerkin was wounded too. Its torn flesh trembled, and it hissed and roared as if it wanted to launch itself back into the attack. But it could not break away from the First Song.

Sinew took a deep breath and began to walk towards the creature. As he did so, he found himself thinking of the children again. Something had changed. They were no longer where they had been a moment ago . . .

He shook himself, and concentrated on the music. He made it sing with longing, with a desire for rolling plains and fat slow cattle. For the sun, hot and glistening, and the huffing of new-born cubs. For slommerkin heaven, just beyond the Dirty Gate.

The slommerkin hissed again, and lashed out with its tusks. Sinew jumped back a step, but his fingers did not miss a note.

'*Come*,' sang the music (twining in and out of the First Song). '*Come to sun-on-the-skin and food-in-the-*

belly. Come to gobble-gobble-liver-and-hearts. Come to eat-all-you-want.'

The slommerkin's tiny eyes blinked. It sank back on its torn haunches and scratched itself thoughtfully. Then, with a shudder, it heaved itself to its feet and began to make its way towards the Dirty Gate.

Sinew followed, with Broo limping beside him. His fingers never paused in their task. *'Come! Come to roll-on-bones! Come to suck-at-marrow!'*

The slommerkin moaned with hunger. The keeper and the brizzlehound drove it onwards, through The Tench, through Lost Children and Dauntless, and across the perilous landscape of Knife Edge. Until at last they came to their destination.

The Dirty Gate lay deep inside the museum, in a long, narrow room with a stone floor and stone walls. There were no exhibits here, no display cases, just cold-hearted stone and, at the far end, the Gate itself, its massive iron strips twisted together like honeycomb.

The slommerkin paused halfway down the room, snuffing the air. Sinew peered past it and saw that the Dirty Gate was open, and that Herro Dan and Olga Ciavolga stood to one side of it, with a small fire burning at their feet.

He added a note of urgency to the song he played. *'Don't stop! Don't tarry! Liver-and-hearts! Marrow-bones!'*

The slommerkin surged down the room. But just as it was about to step through the Gate, Sinew's bleeding fingers slipped. A discord rang out.

The slommerkin hesitated. Its head swung from side to side. It turned around, its little eyes fixed on Herro Dan. It licked its pendulous lips . . .

'No!' cried Olga Ciavolga, and she snatched a burning stick from the fire and threw it, as straight as a spear. The slommerkin squealed with pain. It shuffled backwards through the Dirty Gate, pawing at its nose. Quickly, the keepers threw themselves at the Gate and pushed it shut. Herro Dan shot the bolt, then he took a large key from his pocket and turned it in the lock.

With a groan of exhaustion, Sinew slid down the wall and laid his harp on the floor. Broo flopped beside him.

'Never met anyone who could throw like you can, lass,' said Herro Dan with a shaky laugh.

'Pfft, it was easy.' The old woman smiled, but her face was white. 'Give me something hard to do next time.'

Broo raised his head from his paws. An enormous sigh escaped him. 'Is there anything to eat? I am very hungry.'

'Oh, my dear,' said Olga Ciavolga, bending over him. 'Of course you are hungry. And look at your poor shoulder! Come with me, I will sew you up and feed you. Sinew, you too. We must do something about your hands.'

Sinew nodded but did not move. 'You and Broo go on ahead. I'll follow when I've caught my breath.'

As Olga Ciavolga hurried away, with the brizzlehound limping beside her, Herro Dan eased his old bones down to the floor. 'That was well done, lad,' he said, patting Sinew on the arm.

Sinew yawned. 'I have never in my life played so long and hard. I hope I never have to do such a thing again, but—'

'So do I, lad.'

'But when I was in the middle of it, I sort of *felt* the children.'

'What? *Where?*'

'I don't know. But I think something has happened to them. Something strange.' Sinew drew his torn fingers through the air above his harp, and a single bright note rang out. 'Something *very* strange.'

WARRIOR PRINCESS

Princess Frisia

Frisia, Crown Princess of Merne, slid the bent wire into the lock of her bedchamber door. This wasn't the first time that her bodyguards had locked her in at night. They said it was necessary to keep her safe from assassins. But Frisia had her own ways of getting out . . .

One by one the pins inside the lock slid up and out of the way.

The door cracked open. She listened for the sound of breathing and heard nothing – her bodyguards hadn't yet arrived for duty. Good.

She strapped her sword over the boy's tunic she habitually wore, pulled on a fur robe and crept out into the silent corridor, closing the door behind her. The flagstones were cold, even through her shoes, and a wisp of winter fog had seeped through the walls.

Her hands were cold too. In fact, her whole body was freezing, as if she had just climbed out of an icebound river rather than a warm bed. She shivered and drew her robe closer. All around her, the upper floors of the castle slept.

Frisia hurried past Physician Hoff's apartments, and past the family chapel, where two stone wolves stood guard. She kissed their noses for luck, as she had done ever since she was tall enough to reach them, then she turned the corner and let herself into the apartments that were reserved for the Margrave of Spit and his children.

She could hear movement in one of the bedchambers. She tapped on the door, feeling for the scrap of paper in her coin pocket. Despite the early hour, a maidservant opened the door almost straight away. When she saw the princess, she bobbed a curtsey.

'I am here to see the Young Margrave,' said Frisia, stepping past her.

The maidservant bobbed again. 'He's looking better, Your Highness. He was very cold a while ago, but we put some more wood in the stove and he's warmed up nicely. And the wound is clean.'

Harmut, the Young Margrave of Spit, was asleep in his father's four-poster bed, his head bandaged and the quilts piled to his chin. The stove in the corner of the room gave out a sultry heat.

Frisia peered down at her friend. The maidservant was right, he was looking a lot better. Still, head wounds could be dangerous things. Frisia's great uncle Rulf had ended his days a drooling idiot as the result of such a wound.

There was a creak from the four-poster and Harmut rolled onto his side. 'Gold,' he mumbled.

'What?' said Frisia. She pushed her scabbard out of the way and sat down on the bed. 'Harmut, are you awake?'

The boy's eyes snapped open. 'Frisia? What are you doing here?'

'Were you dreaming of gold?'

'Was I dreaming? I suppose I must have been. Everything was – strange.'

'There'll be plenty of gold when we beat Graf von Nagel,' said Frisia. 'According to our spies, his war chests are bursting. I'll ask Father to let you have third choice of the treasure after him and me, if you like. That is if you're still coming to Halt-Bern with us tomorrow.'

'Why wouldn't I be?' Harmut moved again and winced. His fingers fumbled out from beneath the quilts and found the bandage. He blinked in confusion. 'What's wrong with my head?'

'You were—' Frisia broke off. Some of the fog had crept into her mind, and for a second or two she had the oddest feeling, almost like a voice speaking inside her . . .

(What am I doing here? A castle? What am I doing in a castle?)

Then the fog drew back a little and she said, 'You were wounded during sword practice yesterday.'

'Who hit me?'

'I don't know. We were fighting in a melee with Ser Wilm and my bodyguards. I heard a clang, and you fell—' *(in the water)* '—in the training yard.'

Why was she thinking about water? Why did she suddenly have this voice in her head? *(Cold water . . . Icy water, lapping at my throat . . .)*

She shook herself. It was probably just nerves. She had been trained in the art of war since the day she learned to walk, and had been in several minor battles, but this would be her first proper campaign.

'Are *you* still going to Halt-Bern?' said Harmut.

Frisia stared at him in astonishment. 'Of course I am. Why would I stay behind?'

'I don't know. I just thought—'

Frisia felt a surge of anger. 'You thought *what?*' She jumped to her feet. 'That I'd become a *coward* since you saw me last?'

'No. But I thought— I thought I remembered you saying *Never . . .*' His voice trailed off.

'Nothing would stop me going!' said Frisia fiercely. 'I am the daughter of warriors and the granddaughter of warriors, and it is my *destiny* to see von Nagel beaten. And when he is dead and the crows have stripped the flesh from his carcass, I will bring his skull back to Merne. It will make a nice spittoon for Father.'

Harmut sniffed. 'Ha! Bold words.'

'And they'll be matched by bold deeds.'

The two of them glowered at each other. Frisia had been intending to show him the paper in her coin pocket, but now she changed her mind.

'Harmut?' said a voice from the doorway. A small dark-haired girl in a nightgown blinked sleepily at them. 'Are you better?'

'Hello, Uschi,' said Frisia. 'I'm afraid your brother has lost some of his sense.'

'I've got enough left to fight von Nagel,' muttered Harmut.

Another maidservant appeared behind Uschi, fluttering her hands anxiously. 'The Young Margravine should not be visiting people in her night wear.'

'It's not *people*,' said Uschi. 'It's my *brother*.' She dodged the hands of the maidservant and sat down on Harmut's bed. 'I'm glad you're awake. I wanted to ask you about the voyage to Halt-Bern. Do you think I should take my second-best bow as well as my best one? I don't want—'

Harmut fell back onto his pillow with a groan. 'How many times do I have to tell you, Usch? You're not going. You're too little.'

'Harmut doesn't think *anyone* else should go,' said Frisia nastily. 'He wants to beat von Nagel all by himself and come home a big hero.'

'That's not what I said,' muttered Harmut. 'I just thought—' He closed his eyes. 'My head hurts.'

The first maidservant bustled to his bedside. 'The Young Margrave should try to sleep a little more,' she said, straightening the covers.

Frisia pulled a face and walked out of the room. Uschi followed, saying, 'What are you doing now? Where are you going? Can I come with you?'

'You'll have to get dressed first.'

'Wait here,' said Uschi. 'Don't go without me.' And she disappeared into her bedchamber.

Frisia leaned against the wall, kicking at the heavy tapestry with the heel of her shoe. How *dare* Harmut say such things to her? What could possibly stop her from going to Halt-Bern? It was her destiny . . .

The word echoed in her mind – almost as if she had been in this position before, in another time and place. *Knowing* that she had been born for something important. Only the last time – was it possible? – she had turned her back on it.

She was glad when Uschi came out, dressed in tunic and hose, with a dagger in her belt. Frisia took the scrap of paper from her pocket and flattened it out. 'Look at this. Someone pushed it under my door a little while ago.'

Uschi wrinkled her forehead. 'It looks like mouse scratchings. What's it supposed to be?'

'It's a drawing of the dungeons, I think. See, that's the passage, and there are the cells. Shall we go and see what it's about?'

The two girls hurried down the main staircase to the Memorial Hall of Frisia's great grandfather, Ferdrek III. From there, they slipped through the concealed door that led to the kitchens and saucing rooms. The lower floors of the castle had been awake for some time, and the smell of bacon and pickled herring wafted out to meet them.

As they passed from the saucing rooms into the cellars, Frisia loosened her sword in its scabbard. Immediately, deep inside her, she felt the rising snarl of the royal wolf-sark – the battle madness that flared up whenever a king or queen or princess of Merne unsheathed a weapon.

She pushed it back down. She did not think there was any real danger here. The sword was just for caution.

'Do Kord and Smutz know you're down here?' whispered Uschi. 'Did you show them the note?'

'Of course not. They'd just say it was a ruse to get me out of my room. They'd want to come with me.'

'Well, I suppose that's what bodyguards are for.'

Frisia pulled a face in the darkness. 'I can look after myself.'

'And besides, you've got me,' whispered Uschi.

In the far wall of the cellar, the iron door that led to the dungeon stood ajar. Frisia could see a faint glow through the gap. 'Who's there?' she called softly. 'Show yourself.'

No one appeared, but she heard a whisper, 'Don't *you* go. What if she's not alone? What if she's brought *them* with her?'

'*We'll* go, *we'll* tell her,' said another voice.

'He's not listening,' said a third voice. 'Wilm, dearie, why won't you *listen* to us?'

Frisia grinned at Uschi and the two girls stepped through the door into the middle of a crowd of small, plump women. When they saw the princess, the women made quick curtseys. The hems of their aprons whispered against the floor. Their white linen caps bobbed up and down like daisies in a field.

Beyond the women stood a slim young man of about twenty years old, dressed in the overtunic of a knight of Merne and holding a wax taper. He had blond hair and blue eyes, and he was bowing deeply.

'Ser Wilm,' said Frisia. 'Was it you who sent the drawing?'

She did not expect him to answer. He had taken a vow of silence and his servants, who had raised him from childhood and loved him dearly, always spoke for him.

'Your Highness,' said one of them. 'We did not know if you would come.'

'We thought you might bring nasty Kord,' said another. 'Or Smutz, the big lump.'

Uschi laughed. Frisia said, 'It is just me and the Young Margravine, as you can see. Tell us what has happened.'

Ser Wilm beckoned them towards the crumbling passage that led to the dungeons.

'He wants to show you,' said one of the servants. 'Is that wise, Wilm dearie? Be careful.'

The young knight rolled his eyes at Frisia. 'But what has *happened*?' she said, as she followed him down the stone-lined passage.

'Didn't we tell you, Your Highness?' said a servant, scurrying to catch up. 'It's the duchess. She's been locked up.'

'*What?*' said Frisia. 'But she's the ambassador-in-exile from Halt-Bern. The king would never dishonour her by locking her up!'

'It was not the king,' muttered another servant darkly. 'He is a good man. Hard, but good. He asked us to tell his fate last week, and he paid us for it, which he had no need to do. We think he does not know about the duchess.'

'So who *did* lock her up?' said Uschi.

'Two men came and took her during the night. We were afraid they would take us too, so we hid in the linen cupboard and did not see their faces. We heard the duchess kicking and scratching, and the men swearing at her. She nearly took one of their eyes out.'

The servants tittered in unison.

Frisia hadn't been to the dungeons for years, and she had forgotten how grim and silent they were. The ceiling of the guardroom was so low that Ser Wilm's head brushed against it. Most of the cell doors were open, but one was closed and bolted, with an enormous padlock on it.

'Give me the light,' said Frisia. Ser Wilm handed her the taper, and she held it up to the barred window. At first she could see nothing. Then, in the depths of the cell, something moved.

'Is it her?' whispered Uschi.

'Duchess,' cried Frisia. 'Duchess Orla.'

There was a waft of stale air, and a bundle of black rags rose up from the floor and stalked towards the window. Yellow eyes glared at Frisia from above a beak-like nose. The duchess's black lace mittens gripped the window bars. The iron fetters on her wrists rattled.

Something in Frisia's stomach turned over at the sound. *(Chains. I hate chains . . .)*

'Have you come to laaaaugh at Orla?' croaked the old lady. 'To poke at me as if I were a caaaged beast?'

'No,' said Frisia quickly. 'We've come to get you out.'

There was no sign of the key that would open the cell door. Frisia handed the taper to Uschi then set to work on the padlock with her knife and wire.

The younger girl peered, fascinated, over her shoulder. 'Where did you learn to do that?'

The question rang inside Frisia's head like a sword hitting a breastplate. Her fingers faltered. 'I— I don't know. I suppose someone taught me . . .'

She stared at the bent wire, searching for an answer. She could remember who had taught her how to fight with a sword and shoot with a bow. And how to lead men into battle even though she was so much younger than them and less than half their size. *So why couldn't she remember who had taught her to pick a lock?*

'Are you going to stand there all niiiiight, Princess?' croaked the duchess.

'Sorry,' said Frisia, and she bent to the padlock again.

Within minutes the door was open and the duchess was dragging her chains out into the guardroom. Uschi took a step backwards. The light from the taper flickered on the clammy walls.

'Undo meeee,' croaked the duchess, holding out her bony hands. *(Like claws. Like bird's claws.)*

The fetters were harder to open than the padlock, and Frisia's fingers were slippery with sweat. She beckoned to one of Ser Wilm's servants. 'You will have to hold the knife steady for me.'

The woman's eyes widened and she backed away. 'Pardon me, Highness. I cannot.'

'Do not worry, smaaaall creature,' croaked the duchess. 'I prefer my food dead.'

'But how does it *get* dead?' whispered the servant. 'That's the question, Duchess.'

'Look,' said Frisia impatiently, 'she's not going to eat you, is she?'

Once again the words rang inside her head, as if they were not as absurd as they should have been. The duchess cackled with laughter. The white-capped women whispered to each other in frightened voices. When Ser Wilm stepped forward, they did their best to stop him, but he gently pushed them out of the way.

He wasn't at all afraid. He smiled at the duchess in his usual cheerful manner, then took the knife from Frisia's hand and held it in place while she picked the lock.

The fetters fell to the floor with a clang. The ambassador-in-exile stretched her bony arms wide and flapped them up and down to get the blood flowing. 'Aaaah, that's better,' she said. 'Now, Princess. Taaaake me to your faaather.'

'We had better go to my apartments first,' said Frisia, 'so you can wash. Then we'll go to the king.'

The duchess set off up the passage with her black sleeves billowing. Frisia, Uschi, Ser Wilm and his servants hurried after her.

'Do you think everyone in Halt-Bern talks like that?' whispered Uschi, as they emerged into the Memorial Hall. '"Taaaake me to your faaather."'

'Sshh,' whispered Frisia.

The little party was halfway up the Grand Staircase when something fell from the duchess's hand. The princess bent to pick it up. When she saw what it was, she almost dropped it again. *(A black feather . . .)*

No. No, it wasn't. It was merely one of the old lady's lacy mittens. And yet, Frisia could have sworn . . .

For a moment she had the peculiar feeling that there were *two* people inside her body, instead of one. 'Duchess,' she said, swallowing. 'Here. You dropped your mitten.'

They hurried past the stone wolves, and drew up at last in front of Frisia's door. Her bodyguards had still not arrived at their station, and there was a flash of white under the door that hadn't been there earlier.

One of Ser Wilm's servants fell to her knees. 'Look, Highness. Someone has put a sheet under your door.'

It was not a sheet, Frisia could see that straight away. It was a glass-cloth, of the sort that was used to clean crystal. There were several of them, stuffed along the bottom of her door, filling the gap, so that light could not get in or out.

Deep inside her, a half-remembered conversation swam to the surface. *(Light – or air. Poisoned air . . .)*

The duchess jabbed at the keyhole with her bony hand. 'This has been filled tooooo.'

(Poisoned air . . . Shivers! Assassins!)

Assassins? A chill ran through Frisia. 'The king!' she cried.

Without waiting to see if the others would follow, she began to run. She heard the scrape of Ser Wilm's sword behind her. She turned the corner towards her father's apartments – and almost fell over two of the Royal Guards, lying full-length on the floor, sound asleep and snoring loudly.

She dropped her fur robe and leaped over the guards. The door of the Presence Chamber was wide open and she raced through it, past the enormous throne to the double doors at the far end that led to the King's Gallery. There, another two guards lay on the floor, their helmets crooked, their eyes closed.

'Assassins!' cried Frisia. 'Beware assassins! *Guards!*'

There was an answering shout, and Frisia's body-guards, Kord and Smutz, raced around the corner. But to the princess's horror there was no sign of the other guards who should have come.

'Duchess!' she cried. 'Rouse the castle! The rest of you, with me!'

They ran together down the long gallery, with the portraits of Frisia's warlike ancestors glaring at them from both sides. In his eagerness to protect her, Kord crowded against the princess, slowing her down and almost tripping her.

'Out of my way, fool!' she screamed.

Into the Large Withdrawing Room they raced,

and out the other end. Through the Library and the Small Withdrawing Room. At each door the men who should have been guarding the king lay sleeping or unconscious.

They reached the Royal Bedchamber and Frisia threw herself against the door. It was locked. 'Ser Wilm!'

The young knight ran backwards, then launched himself at the door. The lock rattled, but did not give way. He tried again.

(He can't do it. He's only a little boy . . .)

Frisia shook her head. Where had *that* thought come from? Of *course* Ser Wilm wasn't a little boy! Of *course* he could do it—

There was a splintering sound and the door flew open. As the princess ripped her sword from its scabbard, the chill inside her became a blaze of heat, surging from the soles of her feet to the crown of her head. The wolf-sark *roared* in her throat! The red mist descended upon her, cutting off all further thought.

With a wild battlecry, she launched herself into the king's chamber.

A DAY AND A NIGHT

Pounce

A cloud of foul yellow smoke filled the Royal Bedchamber. Frisia stumbled through it, sword in hand, searching for the assassins. The wolf-sark raged like a furnace inside her. The red mist demanded blood. She no longer knew where she was—

The small, clear voice in her head was like an island of sanity. *(The king! Hurry!)*

Frisia's hand brushed against something. With a monstrous effort, she dragged her mind clear of the red mist – and recognised the silk hangings that enclosed the king's bed. She pushed them aside, and there was Father, sprawled under the bedcovers. His eyes were closed and his face was the colour of gristle.

(Get him out of here!)

The king was a huge man, and it took Kord, Smutz and Ser Wilm to carry him out of the poisoned bedchamber to the clean air of the Library. There they laid him on a daybed under a pile of furs. Frisia knelt beside him, her whole body shaking as the wolf-sark drained out of her.

By now, everyone in the castle was awake. The alarm bell tolled and servants ran hither and thither. Off-duty members of the Royal Guard stumbled into the Library, their boots half-buckled, their faces white with shock. The hunt for the assassins was already underway.

Physician Hoff arrived in her nightgown. 'More furs,' she bellowed, rolling her sleeves up her plump arms. 'Light some torches so I can see what I'm doing. And get those stoves going. We must sweat the poison air out of him.'

'Will he live?' said Frisia.

The physician held a potion to the king's lips. 'Who knows?' she muttered. 'It is in the hands of the gods.'

231

(Flick your fingers. Quickly.)

Frisia did not understand where the strange voice in the back of her mind had come from, or why it was talking to her like this. But it had helped save her father, and so she was willing to trust it. She flicked her fingers. Ser Wilm looked at her curiously.

Physician Hoff had managed to get the king to swallow a very small amount of the potion. The king spluttered and began to cough. His eyes flickered open. 'What is – *cough cough*—' He shook his head, and some of the colour came back into his face.

The physician begged him to drink more, but the king pushed the bowl away. His voice was like the crackling of old parchment. 'What is this – you are feeding me – Hoff? Are you trying to – kill me?'

Physician Hoff's plump face was unreadable. 'I am simply trying to mend you, Your Majesty,' she said.

'Consider me – *cough cough* – mended.' The king tried to raise himself on one elbow, but he was too weak. 'Was it von Nagel's – assassins? Of course it was. The treacherous creatures – they nearly got me this time.' His fierce gaze swivelled to the princess. 'And Frisia – *cough* – saved me? Good. Good. You are your father's daughter.'

He turned back to the physician. 'What was it they used? The smell—'

A woman's voice came from the doorway. 'Burning stink-roses. They drugged the guards and slipped a fire-pan into your chamber.'

The speaker was tall, elegant and extremely thin. Her eyes were dark, and her grey velvet gown was trimmed with rat-skins, lying nose to tail around the neck and wrists.

Frisia had no idea who she was.

'Common stink-roses,' said the woman. 'Who would have thought they could do such harm?' She strolled up to the daybed and kissed the king's pallid cheek. 'I am glad that you are still with us, Ferdrek.'

Physician Hoff cleared her throat. 'The stink-rose, Lady Katerin, lets off poisonous vapours when it is dried and burned.'

Aunt Katerin. Of course. Frisia shook her head. How could she have forgotten? What was *wrong* with her this morning?

The king tried to say something, but he was overtaken by a coughing fit that sounded as if it might tear his lungs out. When he was quiet again, Physician Hoff leaned over the daybed and murmured, 'I recommend just a *little* more of the potion, Your Majesty. And some for the princess as well, in case she breathed in the poison.'

Aunt Katerin sniffed the bowl and wrinkled her nose.

'I cannot imagine *that* doing my brother any good. Take it away, Hoff.'

By now the stoves were packed with wood and the room was growing hot. Frisia could feel the sweat running down her back. At the same time, her hands felt cold again. She looked at Physician Hoff, and at Kord and Smutz, standing to attention on either side of her, and knew that there was something she must remember. Something important. But what was it?

(A day and a night. Be ready for when it stops . . .)

What? wondered Frisia. *When* what *stops?*

'Where is Grand Duke Karl?' growled the king. 'Bring him to me. Bring all of them. There is much to be done – *cough cough* – if the army is to sail for Halt-Bern tomorrow morning.'

'But Your Majesty,' said Physician Hoff. 'Surely you cannot go to Halt-Bern now?'

'No doubt that was the – purpose of this attack,' rasped the king. 'But we are not so – easily beaten. Karl will lead the army in my stead.'

'And I will be there to help him,' said Frisia quickly.

The king grunted. 'Not without me. Not – this time.'

Frisia's heart beat like a war drum in her chest. It was her destiny to fight von Nagel. She *must* go!

'Father,' she said, as calmly as she could, 'the troops are expecting me to be there.'

'Then they will be disappointed,' growled the king. 'But they will fight nonetheless.'

And although she pleaded with him, he would not change his mind.

Frisia had first heard the rules of warfare when she was six years old. Since then, she had come to realise that one of them was more important than all the others put together.

Know your enemy.

The king was fascinated by the fates. He liked to consult them whenever possible, especially on the eve of war. And so, as soon as the grand dukes and margraves were gathered around his daybed, muttering to each other in shock and outrage, Frisia took a deep breath and stepped forward.

'Father, may we have a fate-telling for the campaign ahead?'

The king dragged himself up to a sitting position. 'Good – *cough cough* – idea. Who will do it? The Wilm lad?'

'Yes, Father.' Frisia raised her hand, and Ser Wilm

strode forward, with his servants fluttering around him.

'You will find this – interesting,' said the king to the gathered nobles. 'I had not seen a telling done this way – before last week. It is even better than a goose's entrails.' He waved weakly at Ser Wilm. 'Get on with it.'

Ser Wilm's servants dragged a number of books and manuscripts out of the various cabinets, and laid them open on the long table. Then one of them took Frisia's hand. 'Close your eyes please, Highness, and put your finger on each book, anywhere you please. But do not peek.'

Frisia closed her eyes and stretched out her hand. Once again she had the feeling that she was sharing her body with someone else. And that the other one, the one who was *not* Frisia, had as much riding on the fate-telling as *she* did.

'Thank you, Highness,' said the servant, when Frisia had touched all twelve books. 'You can open your eyes now.'

'Is that it?' growled the Margrave of Numme.

'No, the interesting bit comes next,' said the king.

Ser Wilm handed six of the books back to his servants. The others he moved around according to a pattern that Frisia could not see.

'But this is not the fates,' protested the Margrave of Numme. 'He could turn it any way he wished.'

The king laughed. 'That is the beauty of it. The lad cannot read. He does not know what the fate is, any more than we do. There now, he has finished. Frisia, tell us what it says.'

Frisia approached the books cautiously. Ser Wilm put his finger on the first word she had chosen. 'Fire,' she read.

The second one was *destroy the household*. The third page listed all the weapons in the royal armoury, but the bit that Ser Wilm pointed to was *one longbow, inlaid with silver*. The fourth was an illuminated drawing of a snarling wolf cub. The fifth was another drawing, of a ship this time, sailing towards the horizon with no land in sight. The sixth said *do not hold back*.

'Makes no sense to me,' said the Margrave of Numme.

'It's like a code,' said Frisia. 'You have to work it out.'

The king's face was grey with exhaustion; nothing but his iron willpower still held him upright. But he nodded, pleased. 'Go on.'

'First, the fire,' said Frisia. 'It might mean anything, but it comes just before "destroy the household". I think the household is probably Merne. And the fire is von Nagel, setting out to destroy us.'

The grand dukes rumbled their agreement. Their beards and moustaches wagged and they leaned forward, interested now.

'The longbow is obvious,' said Frisia. 'Our bowmen are one of our greatest strengths. And the emblem of the wolf flies on all our banners.' She paused, looking for something in the last part of the fate-telling that would declare her destiny to the listeners. But she could see nothing.

Her heart sank. 'The ship is— It is our army's voyage to Halt-Bern. And the last one tells us that we must not hold back, we must go with great urgency and fight with all our strength.'

There was a moment of silence, then the king said, 'It is good – to have our plans confirmed. But I confess – I was expecting more. Never mind, there are plenty of other things to – *cough cough cough*—'

All this time Physician Hoff had been hovering in the background with a look of deep disapproval on her face. Now she jumped forward. 'Please, Your Highness, this is too much. You must rest. And take more of the potion, I beg you.'

'I will rest,' growled the king, 'when I am ready.'

He raised his hand, and the gathered nobles knelt to take their battle vows. In rumbling voices they swore that they would fight till every drop of blood in their bodies was gone; that they would slaughter von Nagel and his followers, or cut their own ears off in shame. Then, with a great creaking of leather boots and rattling of swords, they stamped out of the library. Only Grand Duke Karl stayed behind.

Frisia stared at the floor, bitterly disappointed. She had been so sure that the fate would convince the king to let her go to Halt-Bern. But the whole thing had been a waste of time.

In the back of her mind, the strange voice whispered. *(I think there's more. Go deeper . . .)*

The princess's neck prickled. She bent over the table. In the corner of the Library, Ser Wilm's servants put their white caps together and murmured to each other.

'Father,' said Frisia.

The king was lying down now, discussing strategy with the grand duke, and he was clearly annoyed at being interrupted. 'What is it?'

'There is another message here,' said Frisia. Quickly, before the king could dismiss her, she said, 'The first two parts are the same. The fire threatens the household. Von Nagel is setting out to destroy Merne. But the longbow— Look, it's no ordinary longbow. It's inlaid with silver.'

'Pfft,' said the king. 'That means nothing.'

'Perhaps you are right,' said Frisia. 'But when you

239

look at the *next* part of the fate, it becomes clearer. The wolf cub.'

Her father stared at her blankly. 'Don't you see?' said Frisia, her voice trembling with excitement. 'Who is the wolf of Merne?'

'The king, of course,' said Grand Duke Karl.

'Well then, if the king is the wolf, who is the wolf *cub*?'

The room was as silent as the empty dungeons. The king narrowed his eyes and glared at Frisia. She glared back at him. '*I* am,' she said. 'And I carry a bow inlaid with silver rings from our conquered territories on the Faroon Peninsula—'

The king's face reddened. 'Are you trying to twist the words of the fates for your own ends, girl?' he growled.

'No,' said Frisia, standing very straight. 'I am trying to discover their true meaning.'

'And what makes you think that you have found it?'

'Because it makes sense. You were right; we *did* expect more. And this is it. Look at the last two parts of the fate. The ship— I don't think it's a ship after all. I think it's me, sailing away from everything I know. You see, the land is out of sight . . .'

'Hmph,' said the king.

'And then it says, "do not hold back". Perhaps this is

240

the wolf's last chance to beat von Nagel. And you must throw everything against him.' She took a deep breath. 'Including the wolf cub.'

She stopped. There was not a sound except for the crackling of the wood in the iron stove.

Grand Duke Karl cleared his throat. 'I would not be sorry to have her with us,' he said to the king. 'She does not have a quarter of your strength, but when it comes to courage and strategy, she is indeed the wolf's daughter.'

'Hmph,' said the king again, and broke into another fit of coughing.

'Your Majesty—' said Physician Hoff.

'Wait,' growled the king. His eyes were sunk deep in his head by now, and his beard was like dry grass. But he dragged himself back up to a sitting position and turned his fierce gaze on Frisia.

'I expect you to come back with von Nagel's head in a sack,' he rumbled.

Frisia's heart leaped. 'I will, Father. And the ears of his lords.'

The king laughed weakly. 'Ha, that will give me my strength back.'

In the crowded depths of the princess's mind, the strange voice whispered. *(Be ready for when it stops . . .)*

Frisia put her hand on the hilt of her sword. She *was* ready. She didn't know what was coming, but she was as ready as she could be.

'So, wolf cub,' said the king, 'you will board the *Falcon* at first light and sail with the tide. Do you hear me? Well? Speak up.'

Frisia held herself steady. 'I hear you, Father.'

Then she spun on her heel and marched out of the room. In the back of her mind, the voice set up a steady whisper.

(Be ready . . . be ready . . . be ready)

Pounce leaned against a wall and watched the girl from Jewel behaving like an idjit. Walking through doors that weren't there. Talking to people who didn't exist. And all the time with that stuck-up expression on her face as if she thought she was something special.

He poked his tongue out at her, although he knew she couldn't see him. Truth was, he was jealous. 'Don't seem fair,' he muttered to himself, 'that a bunch of visitin' snotties can catch a Big Lie straight off. Not when I been tryin' for years.'

Truth was, it hurt to see Mouse caught up in someone else's Lie. Pounce had been watching him for most of the day and all of the night to make sure people were treating him properly. To make sure nothing bad happened to him.

Now it was nearly dawn, but the rain had held off and the streets were still full of revellers. Pounce was sick of them, sick of the whole Festival. He hadn't told a single lie ever since he'd found that Mouse was missing.

'Idjits,' he muttered, as a group of old men danced past him. 'Cretins. Stupid old fools.'

He turned around and kicked the wall with his bare toes. It hurt terribly, which was good, because it took his mind off the hurt inside him.

Truth was, *he* was the idjit. He should've known that Mouse would try and save the visiting snotties once he found out what was going on. The little boy had always been too soft. And now he was well and truly caught up in Harrow's business.

Just the thought of it made Pounce shiver. 'Don't you touch 'im, Flense,' he whispered. 'Don't you touch my Mousie.'

He heard footsteps and spun around. Cord and Smudge were marching towards him. Pounce caught his breath, then remembered that they couldn't see him.

The two men marched straight past, with their hands in odd positions as if they held weapons. They seemed to be heading towards the harbour. The girl from Jewel walked behind them, waving her hand to an invisible crowd.

Flense came next, right up close as if she didn't want to let the girl out of her sight. And there, trotting after Flense, was Mouse, with his pets lined up along his shoulders.

Pounce felt like grabbing him right there and then and dragging him off home. He would've done it too, except that folk said it was dangerous to pull someone out of a Big Lie before it finished. And he'd already put Mouse in danger. He wasn't going to make it worse.

The skinny old cat strolled behind Mouse with its nose and its tail stuck in the air. The other two visiting snotties followed the cat. And behind the lot of them strutted the big black bird.

Pounce had nearly died of fright the first time he saw that flippin' bird. It was bigger than a dozen pigeons stuck together, and blacker than the blackest sewer. It'd keep you fed for a week if you could get past those claws and that wicked beak. But Pounce wasn't stupid enough to try.

When they'd all passed him, he glanced up at the sky. It was just beginning to lighten, which meant that the Lie would finish very soon. And when it did, Flense, Cord and Smudge were going to chew up those visiting snotties and spit out their bones.

'But they's not gunna chew up Mousie,' whispered Pounce. 'Not if I got any say in it.'

And he turned and ran after his friend.

(Be ready ... be ready ... be ready ...)

The little voice had been whispering in the back of Frisia's mind ever since she woke. But as her carriage approached the waterfront, and the eastern sky lightened with the coming dawn, it grew to a shout.

(BE READY! BE READY!)

The waterfront was bustling. In the grey light, the last of the soldiers were boarding their ships. Quartermasters ticked off lists of food and weapons. Sailors licked their fingers and held them up to test the direction of the wind.

Frisia stared at everyone and everything she passed. She could see nothing out of the ordinary. But the danger was there. She could feel it. And it was getting closer. *Much* closer.

(BE READY!)

The royal procession drew up beside the *Falcon*, the king's flagship. On deck, the captain was waiting to greet the princess. The tide had turned, and he was eager to be gone.

Frisia's nerves were stretched as tight as the ropes that held the ship to the wharf. In the carriage behind her, Physician Hoff, who had insisted on coming to see her depart, was frowning, as if she had a headache.

(BE READY!)

There was a sudden sharp gust of wind across the harbour. Duchess Orla pulled her cloak tighter. A black feather fell to the ground.

'Don't be silly,' Frisia told herself. 'It's just her mitten.'

But the more she looked, the more she saw feathers. Now they were dropping from the duchess's hair. As each one fell, Frisia felt a shock, as if the world she knew was trying to tear itself apart.

No one else seemed to notice. Physician Hoff was rubbing her forehead. Aunt Katerin was licking the back of her hand.

Licking her *hand* . . . ?

Frisia shook her head. The danger was so close now that she could almost smell it. But she still did not know where it was coming from.

Grand Duke Karl had told her about times like this. 'There are moments in any battle,' he had said, 'when you cannot make sense of what is happening. All you can do is trust your instincts. If they tell you to run, then run. If they tell you to attack, then attack. Do not hesitate.'

This wasn't a battle, but the voice inside Frisia was shouting. *(Run!)*

Run where?

(To the ship.)

Frisia beckoned to Kord. 'We will board immediately. Tell the others.'

As her bodyguard walked away, Frisia grabbed her bow and quiver from the carriage. 'Uschi,' she said. 'You're coming with us. Harmut, get her onto the ship.'

Harmut stared at her, startled. 'No, she's not going.'

'Don't argue,' said Frisia. 'I am your princess and I *order* her to go!'

Uschi poked her tongue out at her brother. 'There, you see?'

'Here, put these in my cabin,' said Frisia, handing the bow and quiver to the younger girl. 'Quickly.'

The air was getting lighter by the minute. There was an odd pain behind Frisia's eyes, as if her thoughts were trying to twist themselves into a different shape.

(BE READY ... BE READY ...)

Ser Wilm was standing beside his carriage, surrounded by his servants. When Frisia ran towards them they swarmed around her, crying out in high voices.

'Your Highness, we want to go with him!'

'We've looked after him since he was a baby!'

'Who will watch out for him if we're not there?'

Frisia was operating purely on instinct now, hardly knowing what she was going to say before she said it. 'Ser Wilm. Do your servants have anything that could cut the ropes that tie the *Falcon* to the wharf?'

Ser Wilm looked hard at her. Around him, a dozen voices fell silent. A dozen pairs of eyes focused on Frisia with sudden interest. A dozen bone-handled knives slid out of purses and sleeves.

'They must do it quickly, and no one must see them,' said Frisia. She wasn't sure who she meant by 'no one', but Ser Wilm nodded.

'Does this mean we are going with him?' whispered one of the servants.

'Yes,' said Frisia.

They tried to thank her, but she cut them off and pushed them towards the ship.

'Aunt Katerin!' she shouted. 'Duchess Orla! Please get on board!'

'But I am not coming with you,' said Aunt Katerin.

'You are now,' said Frisia grimly, and she grabbed her aunt's arm and dragged her to the bottom of the gangplank.

Back at the carriages, Physician Hoff was deep in

conversation with Kord and Smutz. Frisia opened her mouth to summon them . . .

(No!)

A chill ran through the princess, and for a moment she could not move. Was *that* where the danger was coming from? The castle physician? Her personal guards?

Suddenly everything made sense. No wonder the assassins had managed to get so close to the king!

She gripped the hilt of her sword and the wolf-sark rose up hot and terrible inside her. She took a step towards Physician Hoff. Her head throbbed. The eastern horizon was so bright that she could barely look at it.

(Run!)

With a great effort, she spun around and leaped up the gangplank. The captain was still standing there, but there was something bloodless and unreal about him. When she shoved past him he hardly noticed.

'Harmut, Uschi,' snapped Frisia. 'Something is about to happen. Be ready.'

Ser Wilm's servants were busy sawing through the two ropes that tied the *Falcon* to the wharf. Aunt Katerin was sitting on the bare boards of the deck, licking her hand and wiping it across her hair. Duchess Orla was climbing the rigging that surrounded the mainmast. Her black cloak flapped around her. Her bony hands gripped the ropes like claws.

Frisia felt horribly dizzy. The air around her was fizzing so violently that the whole wharf shimmered. She heard a squeak from Ser Wilm's servants as the bow rope parted and the front end of the ship swung away from the wharf. With a loud splash, the gangplank tumbled into the harbour.

As if in a dream, Frisia saw Kord's head jerk up. He shouted to Smutz and Physician Hoff, and the three of them began to run towards the ship.

At that moment, the first ray of morning sunlight touched the top of the mast. And the whole world burst open like a bubble.

THE HUNTERS

She had no idea who she was. All she knew was that she lay on the wooden deck of a ship, gasping with shock. Around her, everything was chaos. A boy with a bandaged head was leaning over the rail, vomiting. A girl was crying silently. In the stern, another boy, a much smaller one, stared at his hands as if he couldn't work out who they belonged to.

She heard a harsh croak overhead. An enormous black bird

The Bandmaster

hung upside down from the rigging, its great wings fluttering helplessly. Beneath it a grey-spotted cat snarled and spat.

Who was she?

Frisia?

No . . .

Who, then?

She tried to stand up and the world spun. A different name presented itself to her.

Goldie.

She was . . . Goldie someone . . .

Goldie— Goldie Roth!

With an enormous effort, she dragged herself to her feet and peered around the little deck. She was on the *Piglet*! How did she get there?

And then she remembered. The Festival . . . Pounce's treachery . . . Guardian Hope . . . the Big Lie!

She stumbled to the rail, half-expecting to see the ancient harbour of Merne still spread out in front of her. But Merne was gone, and so were the old-fashioned carriages and the Royal Guards. In their place were the busy docks of Spoke.

And there was Guardian Hope, sitting on the ground, looking sick. But Cord— Cord was staggering towards the ship with his pistol in his hand and Smudge close behind him.

In the back of Goldie's mind a voice cried, *The stern rope!*

Goldie almost fell over with astonishment. That was *Frisia's* voice! What was the princess's voice doing inside her head?

With her thoughts whirling, she raced down the deck to the stern of the *Piglet*. Something whacked against her leg and she glanced down. Frisia's sword was there too!

Goldie swallowed. No time to think about it, not now! 'Out of the way!' she cried, and half a dozen white mice leaped off the stern rope and dived into Mouse's jacket.

As Goldie drew the sword from its sheath, heat surged up inside her, so that she felt as if she was on fire. She raised the sword in both hands, then slashed downwards. With a loud *twang*, the rope parted and the *Piglet* slid away from the wharf.

Too late! Cord and Smudge had leaped across the gap and were clinging to the netting.

'Morg!' screamed Goldie. 'Toadspit!'

There was an answering shout as Toadspit ran towards her, with Morg flapping above him. Cord took one hand off the netting and fired his pistol twice. Morg squawked, and threw herself high into the air. Toadspit dived for cover behind the deckhouse.

The fire inside Goldie burned from her heels to the crown of her head. Something *roared* in her throat, and a red mist descended upon her, so thick and murky that she no longer knew where she was. All she could think of was blood. All she could see was the enemy in front of her, flinging his leg over the side of the ship.

In a mad fury, she raised the sword again . . .

Something brushed her arm. She swung around. *Who DARES touch me?*

She saw Mouse's white, terrified face and tried to stop. But the sword had taken on a life of its own. It sliced through the air towards the little boy!

Goldie fought the sword with all her strength. She fought the fire and the red mist. She *clawed* her way towards the tiny speck of normality that still lay deep within her . . .

The heavy sword stopped, a hair's breadth from Mouse's neck.

For a moment Goldie could not move. Inside her, Frisia's voice hissed furious instructions. *Kill the boarders! NOW!*

With a cry of revulsion, Goldie threw the sword as far away as she could. As it clattered to the deck, Cord and Smudge surged over the rail.

Cord didn't waste a second. He grabbed Goldie and held his pistol to her head. 'Hey, Toadboy,' he shouted.

'Come 'ere. And bring yer sister.'

There was a silence – a *terrible* silence. Goldie looked up in time to see Toadspit shuffle around the side of the deckhouse. His head drooped, his bandage was awry and all the fierce stubbornness that made him who he was seemed to have drained out of him. Even when he was unconscious in the sewer, he had not looked so – so *lost*.

Goldie jammed her bruised knuckles against her mouth. Her legs were shaking uncontrollably. The ship rocked in the swell.

'I said, bring yer sister,' snarled Cord.

Toadspit blinked, as if he had only just realised that someone was talking to him. He raised a trembling hand. He pointed to the gap in the rail where the gangplank had been. 'She fell,' he croaked. 'The bullet— You missed me – and hit her. She fell – in the water. She's – gone.'

His voice broke. A tear rolled down his face. He sank to his knees and began to sob. From somewhere in the clouds high overhead, a harsh voice echoed, 'Go-o-o-ne. Go-o-o-o-o-o-ne.'

Goldie stared at Toadspit, trying to see—

'No,' she whispered. 'Not Bonnie.' And she too began to cry.

'Show me,' said Cord.

'There's nothing to see,' mumbled Toadspit.

'I said, *show me*!' And Cord belted Toadspit across the head with the back of his hand. A trickle of blood seeped from under Toadspit's bandage.

The three children stumbled along the deck at gunpoint to where Bonnie had stood a moment before. The cat crouched next to the covered dinghy, watching them. Cord scanned the deck, then bent down and peered suspiciously at a streak of blood on the boards.

'Could be yours,' he said to Toadspit.

'Don't think so, Cord,' said Smudge, who was squinting over the rail at the water. 'Look at that black thing floatin' down there. It's a shoe, a little 'un. Looks like the ones the girl was wearin'. Want me to fetch it up?'

'Nah, don't bother.' Cord's lips drew back from his teeth in a vicious smile. 'So she's dead, eh? Oh dear. What a pity.'

'My little sister,' whispered Toadspit. 'My poor little sister.'

Cord straightened up, his smile gone, his face as tight as a wire. 'Search 'em, Smudge,' he said. 'Then take us back to the wharf. We don't wanna keep Flense waitin'.'

Smudge searched the two boys. But when he came to Goldie he hesitated. 'Hey, Cord. Is she still a princess?'

'Don't be stupid,' hissed Cord. 'Search 'er, or you'll feel me fist.'

Smudge patted Goldie's pockets gingerly and found Toadspit's knife. His eye fell on the sword and he picked it up. 'Hey, look what I got! If that demon cat comes near me I'm gunna slit its gullet.'

Cord whacked him across the ear. 'Get below, ya moron. Start the engine. Bring us back to the wharf.'

'Ow!' said Smudge, looking reproachfully at the other man. 'Ya didn't need to do that.'

He disappeared below deck. A moment later there was a hiss of gas and the engine rumbled to life. Smudge came back up, still clutching the sword, and took the tiller. The *Piglet* began to turn.

Cord shoved the children up against the mainmast, then backed towards the rail, pointing his pistol at them. From the clouds above, Goldie heard a mournful, fading cry. 'Go-o-o-o-o-ne.'

She gripped Toadspit's arm, as if she was having trouble standing up on her own. It was not so far from the truth. Her fingers tapped out a name. *'Bonnie?'*

'Below,' signed Toadspit. *'Hiding.'*

Goldie let out her breath in a long sigh. She had hoped desperately that it was a trick. But Toadspit had been so convincing that even suspicious Cord had believed him. And the shoe had worried her . . .

'*Blood?*' she signed.

'*Mine.*'

'*Shoe?*'

'*Bonnie's. Threw it.*'

The ship bumped against the wharf. 'Hey, Flense,' shouted Cord over his shoulder. 'Come and give us a hand. And watch out for that stinkin' bird. It's still around somewhere.'

Guardian Hope scrambled over the rail, puffing and grumbling. 'You took your time. *And* they nearly got away. Where's—' She caught sight of Goldie and her mouth fell open. '*Golden Roth!* I should have known!'

She stomped forward until her furious face almost touched Goldie's. 'Still interfering in the Fugleman's business, I see,' she hissed. 'Well, this is the last time, I promise you that. The *very last time!*'

She glared at Toadspit too, and Mouse. 'Where's the other girl, Bonnie?' she snapped.

Cord pointed to the water. 'I shot 'er.'

Guardian Hope's face seemed to swell. 'You idiot! What are they going to think when they find her with a bullet in her?'

Cord pretended not to hear the question. He took a splinter of wood from his pocket and began to pick his teeth.

'Well?' demanded Guardian Hope.

Cord's eyes glittered. He spat on the deck, right next to Guardian Hope's foot. 'You don't know these waters real good, do ya, Flense? There's a shark nursery out there.' He nodded towards the mouth of the bay. 'Me an' me brothers used to fish it when we was snotties. Ya chuck in a bit of bait and next thing ya know they're all round the boat. That girl'll be nothin' but bones by now.'

'*Will* she?' said Guardian Hope, with a thoughtful expression on her face. 'Will she indeed?'

Goldie glanced at Toadspit. There was no need to say anything. They could both see what was being planned for them. They must escape, and they must do it quickly.

But escape was looking more and more unlikely. Guardian Hope tied the children to the mainmast, tugging at the knots to make sure they were secure.

'Smudge,' she said, 'keep us next to the wharf. Cord, I have some new instructions for you.'

As Cord followed Guardian Hope to the rail, a familiar sound drifted to Goldie's ears.

Drums. A bombardon. A trombone playing out of tune.

'It's the band,' she whispered. 'The Festival is still going.'

'What band?' breathed Toadspit.

'Look. There!'

The musicians were shuffling along the wharf towards the *Piglet*. Their playing was as bad as ever, but the crowd following them didn't seem to care. Goldie saw someone throw half a dozen buns. Sweetapple dived after them and so did a group of masked snotties. The music stopped. The bandmaster grabbed one of the snotties and shouted at him. The boy seemed to be arguing. Or maybe pleading.

Goldie felt Mouse stiffen beside her. 'What?' she whispered.

Mouse shook his head. Nothing.

As the band drew level with the *Piglet*, Cord's jaw twitched. He muttered something to Guardian Hope, and leaped over the rail onto the wharf.

The bandmaster had been bouncing along with his mask pushed up on his forehead. Now he stopped in his tracks. Sweetapple bumped into him. Dodger bumped into Sweetapple. They began to complain – then they too saw Cord. The music faltered and died. The crowd melted away, as if people could see there was going to be trouble and didn't want any part in it. Only the snotties lingered curiously in the background, their masks turned towards the bandmaster.

He was staring at Cord with a look of terror on his face. Goldie remembered his desperate words the last time she saw him. *'You've signed my death warrant, and that of all my fellows!'*

It was true, she realised. The musicians had been an important part of the diversion when she rescued Bonnie and Toadspit. They hadn't *known* they were a diversion, not until it was too late. But who would believe that? Certainly not Cord.

In the back of Goldie's mind, Frisia's voice whispered, *A warrior always pays her debts.*

Cord pushed past Dodger and grabbed the bandmaster's arm. The bandmaster sagged, as if all the air had gone out of him. With a yellow smile, Cord raised his pistol . . .

'Hey, you,' shouted Goldie. The bandmaster's head jerked in fright.

It's still the Festival, Goldie reminded herself. *Everything I say has to be back to front.*

'Thank you *so* much for helping me,' she cried through gritted teeth. 'You were *so* kind. All that information you gave me.' She rolled her eyes in disgust. 'It was *extremely* valuable. In fact, it's got nothing to do with why we ended up here.'

The bandmaster's mouth formed an 'O' of surprise. Cord was taken aback too. Goldie could see his confusion.

The bandmaster recovered first. He straightened his

coat and sneered at Goldie. 'Pleased to have been able to help you, my dear. I, of course, am *quite* willing to betray my former colleagues. And I'm *terribly* sorry to see that you've got your comeuppance.'

Cord sucked his teeth thoughtfully. Guardian Hope leaned over the side of the ship, her face a picture of outrage. 'What's this? He *betrayed* us? And now he's *boasting* about it? Give him a good whipping, Cord, for playing false with his betters. Then kill him.'

The bandmaster shot her a look of sheer loathing. But Cord spat on the dock and shook his head. 'It's just Festival talk, Flense. Don't worry about it.' And he thumped the bandmaster on the arm in a more-or-less friendly fashion, and turned away.

The bandmaster hesitated, then lunged after him, his chains rattling. 'Going on a journey, Cord? We didn't get much food this morning. Awful rubbish, most of it. I'd hate to give you some. A few bags of nasty little pastries for the trip, maybe? I didn't smell rabbit in some of them. You always disliked rabbit, if I remember rightly.'

He glanced up at Goldie and she thought she saw the ghost of a wink.

'Nah, don't want any,' said Cord, obviously pleased.

'Ho, boys!' shouted the bandmaster. 'I don't need a few of you to carry some provisions on board ship for me.'

The masked snotties surged forward in a mass, pushing

each other out of the way. Old Snot, the bombardon player and Dodger each took a bag from underneath their coats and reluctantly handed them over.

'Steal as many as you like, lads,' said the bandmaster to the snotties. 'I'm sure Cord here won't mind. He's got a nature as sweet as a butterfly's kiss.'

Cord bared his teeth. The snotties laughed but kept their fingers out of the bags.

Goldie could feel Mouse shaking beside her. Her blood surged in her veins. The bandmaster was up to something, she was sure of it. Perhaps there was something in the bags. A message. A weapon.

As the boys scrambled over the *Piglet*'s rail, the band struck up a jaunty tune. Guardian Hope glared at the musicians. 'We're wasting time!' she shouted.

No one took any notice of her. Cord showed the boys where to stow the bags. The band played louder. The boys began to dance.

Within seconds, the deck of the ship was swirling with noise and movement. There were snotties everywhere, shouting and leaping and dancing. Goldie couldn't keep track of them. The cat slunk behind the covered dinghy, out of reach.

Guardian Hope's face was blotchy with rage. 'That's *enough*,' she shouted. 'Stop this nonsense or I'll see you *all* whipped.'

Still they ignored her. Goldie saw her take a small pistol from her pocket and point it at the sky.

The shot, louder than a thunderflash, stopped the dance in its tracks. The snotties cowered against the rail. Down on the wharf, the band members froze, their lips trembling on their instruments.

But before Guardian Hope could spit out the angry words that hovered on her lips, the air around the ship began to hum and swirl.

Smudge's slab face lit up like a candle. 'It's a Big Lie!' he cried. 'I can feel it. Someone's gunna get a Big Lie!'

He was right. Goldie could feel it too. The Festival was still going and there were still Big Lies on the loose. No one had called *this* one, but it had come nonetheless.

'Who's it for? Is it me?' cried Smudge. 'Oh, Bald Thoke, please let it be me!'

Goldie could see the same longing in the eyes of Cord and the snotties. Only Guardian Hope looked annoyed by the interruption. 'We haven't got time—' she began.

The twisting, curling air swooped past her, wrenching whatever she was going to say next out of her mouth. The edge of the wharf sparkled. The bandmaster squeaked in surprise.

'Quick, Cord,' shouted Smudge. 'Ask me a question.'

'Don't be stupid,' muttered Cord. 'It's not you. It's them.'

He pointed towards the musicians, who were bathed in a swirl of flickering possibility. Sweetapple was standing on tiptoe, laughing and crying at the same time, 'It's us! It's us!' Old Snot's toothless mouth was trying to frame a question but, like most of the band, he was too overcome to speak.

Only Dodger had the wits to turn to the bandmaster and cry, 'Who are we? Quick, before it goes. *Who are we?*'

The bandmaster was as stunned as the rest of them. 'We're— We're—' he stammered. His head swivelled this way and that, searching for inspiration. Goldie saw his eyes fall on Guardian Hope, who was also Flense, the woman who had had him whipped . . .

He bared his teeth in a vengeful grin. 'We're hunters,' he cried. 'Free and mighty hunters. And there—' he raised his baton and pointed straight at Guardian Hope '—*there* is our prey!'

With a loud crash, the shackles and chains fell from his ankles, and from the ankles of all his people. He grew taller, and more alert. Sweetapple's limp disappeared. Dodger and the hairy trumpeter bristled with strength. Even Old Snot put down his drum and straightened up, as lithe and energetic as a twenty-year-old.

But that was not all. Having lived through a Big Lie herself, Goldie could see into the very heart of this one. She could see the faint haze around each of the hunters, which seemed to make them even taller and stronger, so that they reminded her of the heroes from the *really* old stories. She could see the furs they wore, and the massive hounds that prowled around them like long-legged wisps of smoke.

Guardian Hope had changed too. She was bigger than the hounds, and her head tilted under a huge rack of antlers. She sniffed the air and snorted.

The bandmaster's head shot around. He pointed towards the *Piglet*.

With a muscular grace, Sweetapple raised her trombone – which was looking more like a spear with every passing moment – and began to stalk towards the ship. Dodger followed, a few steps behind. Goldie held her breath.

Guardian Hope lifted one great cloven hoof and put it down again. She shook her antlers. Then, without warning, she leaped over the rail and began to gallop down the wharf.

The bandmaster raised a shadowy bugle and blew. The hounds yelped and tore after Guardian Hope. With a roar, nearly all of the musicians followed them. Only Dodger stood firm, one eye shut, sighting along his trumpet at the fleeing prey. His right hand drew back. Goldie thought she heard a distant *thwang*, like an arrow being loosed in someone else's dream.

Guardian Hope staggered and fell. But before the hounds could catch her, she dragged herself to her feet again and limped around the end of a warehouse. The hunters and the hounds raced after her, yodelling with the thrill of the chase, and the Big Lie disappeared around the corner and out of sight.

The whole thing had happened so quickly that Goldie was dumbstruck. She looked at Toadspit, and he looked back at her, equally shocked.

Behind them, Cord chortled. 'Hee hee hee, poor old Flense. She weren't expectin' *that*, were she?'

'D'ya think we should go after 'em?' said Smudge uncertainly. 'Try and help 'er?'

'Try and help *Flense*? When did she ever help us? Nah, I reckon she's done for. Which means *I'm* second-in-command now. And I say we carry out Harrow's orders. No more, no less. Then we go to Jewel to collect our pay.'

Cord shooed the snotties over the rail. 'Rightio, Smudge, take us out into the bay.'

As Smudge shifted the tiller, the *Piglet* slid slowly away from the wharf. 'Where are we goin', Cord?'

Cord grinned, his eyes as hard and bright as bullets.

'We're goin' back to my boyhood. We're gunna introduce this lot—' he pointed his chin at Goldie, Toadspit and Mouse '—to the shark nursery.'

THE SHARK NURSERY

T here was no weapon inside the bags that the bandmaster had sent on board. Nor was there a message. There didn't seem to be anything in them except pastries. Goldie watched as Cord ate his way through them, his jaw working with a mad and violent purpose.

'Um— Cord?' said Smudge, eyeing the children uneasily. 'Are we really gunna – you know?'

'Yep,' said Cord, through a mouthful of pastry.

Bonnie

'All three of 'em? Do we 'ave to?'

''Oo's the boss 'ere, Smudge? You or me?'

'You, Cord!'

'And don't you forget it.'

As the *Piglet* surged towards the edge of the bay, the wind began to pick up and the clouds lowered. Above the children's heads the rigging cracked against the mast.

Goldie stared at the clouds, hoping to catch some sign of Morg. Had the slaughterbird been driven away by Cord's gun? Or was she still up there somewhere?

Whichever it was, she could not help them. The children were at the mercy of a man who was about to throw them to the sharks.

Right up until that minute, Goldie had been able to hold her growing fear at bay. But now it sidled up to her and showed its pointed teeth. Her lip trembled. She closed her eyes, unable to bear the thought of what was coming.

Deep inside her, Frisia's voice whispered, *A warrior learns to see past her fear.*

Goldie swallowed. Herro Dan had once said something similar. Something about treating your fear politely, and doing what you had to do in spite of it.

She took a deep breath. 'Mouse,' she whispered. 'Could your pets chew through my ropes?'

270

The small boy nodded.

'Mine too,' murmured Toadspit.

Mouse whistled softly, and the front of his jacket rippled. Tiny feet ran down Goldie's arm. The ropes around her chest twitched.

Goldie leaned back against the mast, breathing hard. So. It looked as if they could get free of their ropes. But what then? They were still trapped. Cord had his pistol; Smudge had Frisia's sword. They were both grown men and very strong, and there was no way that the children could beat them in a direct fight.

In the back of her mind Frisia whispered, *Know your enemy . . .*

Cord brushed the last of the crumbs from his lips. Then he stood up and stretched until his joints cracked. 'Better let them sharks know we're comin',' he said.

He lurched towards the children. Mouse hummed under his breath, and his pets ran down the mast and disappeared. Goldie stood as straight as she could, hoping desperately that Cord wouldn't notice the half-chewed ropes.

But Cord didn't even glance at the two older children. Instead, he untied Mouse, scruffed him by the neck of his jacket and began to drag him towards the ship's rail.

For one terrible moment, Goldie thought that Cord

was going to throw the little boy overboard, right there and then. She cried out in protest at the same time as Toadspit shouted, 'No!'

The rigging above their heads rattled. The covered dinghy squawked in its cradle. The cat peered out from behind it and hissed.

Cord picked up a bucket and thrust it into Mouse's hand. When the boy flinched away from the smell, Cord whacked him across the ears. 'Toss that muck over the side,' he said. 'A bit at a time.'

Mouse didn't move. Cord took out his pistol and tapped it against the little boy's cheek. 'Or if you'd rather,' he said, 'I could toss *you* over.'

Slowly Mouse dipped his fingers into the bucket, pulled out a handful of fish guts, and flung them over the ship's rail. Cord's jaw did a furious little dance, as if he was disappointed not to have an excuse to kill someone. The cat slunk out from behind the dinghy and crouched at Goldie's feet. The mice renewed their assault on the ropes.

Goldie felt a spot of rain on her face, and looked up. The clouds were drawing in and the morning was growing darker. In the back of her mind, Frisia's voice whispered, *Sometimes the best place to hide is in the midst of the enemy's camp.*

'What?'

Sometimes the best place to hide . . .

Goldie looked at the clouds again, at the way they shadowed the deck. *Oh*, she thought. *Of course!*

She leaned towards Toadspit. 'Imitation of Nothingness,' she breathed.

Toadspit stared at her. 'But what's the—' Then he, too, understood.

At first, Goldie found it almost impossible to settle her mind. Fear needled at her. The ship surged up the face of a wave and plunged down the other side. Her ropes twitched under the onslaught of half a dozen tiny sets of teeth.

Then, just as her mind was at last becoming still, something scraped against the side of the ship. Mouse yelped and leaped back from the rail.

A red spot showed on each of Cord's cheeks. He laughed viciously. 'Looks like the nice sharkies are keen to make yer acquaintance, boy. Why don't ya say 'ullo to 'em? Go on. Lean over the rail and send 'em yer best regards.'

Mouse cowered away from him.

'I said, lean over the rail!'

The little boy shot a look of sheer terror at Goldie. She looked back helplessly. Beside her, Toadspit shifted his weight as if he was bracing for a fight. 'Go on, Mouse,' he called. 'Tell them we're going to have shark stew for dinner tonight.'

'Brave words, Toadboy,' sneered Cord. 'I betcha don't sound so clever when you're slidin' down a shark's gullet.'

Mouse took a shaky step towards the rail and leaned over the side. 'Now,' whispered Toadspit. 'While Cord's watching him.'

Goldie closed her eyes and did her best to block out everything – the ship, the sharks, Mouse's fear, her own dread of what was coming. She drew in a deep breath and let it out again.

I am nothing. I am the wind in the rigging . . .

Her mind began to drift outwards. She could feel the quick heartbeats of the mice, like sparks encircling her body. And the cat, glowing like a hot coal on the deck beside her.

I am the smell of the sea. I am the taste of salt water . . .

She could feel Bonnie, crouched in a corner of the hold, her mind fierce and bright. And Toadspit, and Mouse, and Cord and Smudge—

And— And someone else! There was *someone else* on the *Piglet*! Someone hiding in the dinghy. But who was it? And why . . .

Another shark scraped against the hull. Goldie could feel its hunger, as pitiless as a sword's edge. She shuddered. And opened her eyes.

Toadspit was no longer there beside her.

Or at least, he *was* there, but not one person in ten thousand could have seen him.

Smudge's shocked cry came sooner than she expected. 'Hey, Cord, they're— They're *gone!*'

Goldie felt Toadspit quiver beside her. She forced herself to breathe so slowly that the air itself hardly knew she was there. As Cord's boots pounded across the deck, she stood as still as death.

I am nothing. I am the memory of nothing. I am the smell and taste of nothing . . .

Cord skidded to a halt some distance away. His pistol was in his hand and his teeth were bared. 'They musta had another knife. You idjit, Smudge! I told ya to search 'em.'

'I did, Cord. I promise I did.'

Cord's sharp face swung from side to side, searching the deck. Goldie felt his eyes pass over her. Once. Twice.

I am nothing . . . nothing . . . nothing . . .

'They gotta be 'ere somewhere,' muttered Cord. 'Shouldn't be too hard to find 'em. And when I do—'

He strode up the deck, kicking at the folded sails with his foot. When he came to the bow he turned around and glared at everyone and everything. Mouse shrank back against the rail.

'Wherever yez are, ya little snots,' Cord shouted, 'I'm

gunna find yez. Yez're gunna be sorry that yez tried to mess with me.'

Suddenly the ropes around Goldie loosened. Tiny paws scampered down the mast and disappeared. The cat began to clean itself with a calm tongue.

Goldie drew in a silent breath. Toadspit was free too. She felt him slip away from the mast.

'Cord?' said Smudge, shaking his big head uneasily. 'I *did* search 'em. I don't think they *did* 'ave another knife.'

Cord ignored him. He was working his way down the other side of the deck now, poking into every corner. Goldie saw Mouse glance at the dinghy, his face a mask of terror.

'I dunno how they got outta them ropes.' Smudge rolled his eyes. 'D'ya think it's some sorta magic? Some sorta *demon* magic? Do ya?'

Know your enemy.

Very carefully, Goldie squatted down until her mouth was right next to the cat's ear. 'Cat,' she breathed. 'We need something that looks like magic. Now.'

For a moment the cat didn't move. Then it stood up, yawned hugely and began to stalk towards the deckhouse with its ragged tail held high.

Cord kicked over a barrel with his foot. Nothing. With a grimace of fury he strode towards the dinghy. But just as his hand gripped the tarpaulin, there was a horrified yelp from the deckhouse. 'Cord! It's lookin' at me!'

Cord stopped. 'What are ya talkin' about?'

'The demon cat! It's lookin' at me!'

The cat was indeed looking at Smudge. It stalked towards him, its fierce eyes fixed on his face. He let go of the tiller and backed away, sword in hand. Goldie braced herself against the mast. The ship lurched, and Smudge fell over.

Immediately a dozen white mice swarmed out of the hatch behind him, each one with a scrap of old gazette in its teeth. They dropped the bits of paper beside his head and scuttled away again.

'Cord,' groaned Smudge. 'It's magic. I told ya.'

'Don't be stupid,' snapped Cord. 'You've seen them mice before. They belong to the snotty, the little 'un.'

Smudge shook his head. 'The cat made 'em do it. It's magic.' He picked up one of the scraps of paper and his mouth fell open. 'Look what it says. *Death*. And this one. *Died*. And *this* one. *Dead man*. It's me fortune, Cord. They've told me fortune. I'm gunna die. Just like Flense.'

Cord snarled, 'It's not *you* who's gunna die, idjit. It's the *snotties*. Pull yerself together.'

Goldie drifted closer to Smudge. As she passed him, she whispered in his ear, 'Poor Smudge, dead and gone.'

Smudge flinched and leaped to his feet. 'Who said that?'

'Who said what?' growled Cord.

A shadow drifted past Smudge on the other side. Goldie heard Toadspit whisper, 'Deeeaaad and goooone.'

Smudge jabbed at the air with his sword. 'Don't you come near me,' he said in a quavering voice. 'I don't want no ghostie magic near *me*.'

Cord strode down the deck and grabbed the big man by the arm. 'What's the matter with ya, talkin' to thin air? You smarten yerself up, Smudge. We got a job to do 'ere, and we're gunna do it. Now git that tiller and bring us back on course or I'll chuck *you* overboard.'

Smudge gulped. His eyes rolled in his head, and he gripped the sword with white fingers. But Cord's words had had their desired effect. He took the tiller again, one-handed, and brought the *Piglet* back on course.

Cord watched him for a minute or two, then disappeared around the back of the deckhouse, muttering to himself and poking his pistol into every corner.

As soon as he had gone, Goldie drifted closer to the tiller. 'Hooow did Smuuuudge diiiieee?' she whispered. 'Hooooow did he diiiieeee?'

'Shut up,' mumbled Smudge. 'I'm not listenin' to ghosties. Cord says you're not real.'

'Hooow did he diiiiieeee?' crooned Toadspit.

The cat flicked its tail and flattened its ears against its skull. 'Drooooowned,' it wailed.

'No!' cried Smudge.

'Yer testin' me patience, Smudge,' roared Cord from behind the deckhouse.

There was a squeal from the rigging. Goldie looked up. The mice were strung along the lines like little white signal flags. 'Dreeewn, dreeewn, dreewn,' they squeaked in chorus.

At the same time there was a clap of wings overhead and Morg dropped out of the clouds. 'Dro-o-o-o-o-o-o-o-wned,' she cawed, and her great claws slashed at the air near Smudge's head.

Smudge waved his sword wildly. Cord fired a shot, but the slaughterbird was already gone.

'Cord!' cried Smudge. 'We gotta turn back. I'm gunna drown. The ghosties said so!'

'It's not ghosties; it's the *snotties*,' hissed Cord through gritted teeth. 'Where are they? They gotta be 'ere somewhere.'

'I'm gunna drown!'

'When I catch 'em,' said Cord, 'you can stick that stupid sword through 'em. Then you'll see they're not ghosties.'

Goldie crept up behind the big man. 'Pooor Smuuuuudge,' she crooned. 'Stabbed himself with a swooooord.'

Smudge spun around. He raised the sword, then stared at it uncertainly. His hand shook. On the other side of him, Toadspit whispered, 'With a swooooord.'

'Swooooooord,' wailed the cat, its tail thrashing from side to side.

A black feather drifted down and landed on the deck in front of Smudge. 'Swo-o-o-o-o-o-o-rd,' cried Morg from inside the clouds.

'Sweeerd, sweeerd,' squeaked the mice, jumping up and down in the rigging.

'No!' cried Smudge, and he flung the sword away with all his strength.

As it hit the deck, someone screamed. Goldie swung around. While she and Toadspit had been tormenting Smudge, Cord must have crept past them and grabbed Mouse. Now the little boy teetered on the ship's rail with his legs dangling over the side and his face as white as chalk. Cord held him by one arm.

Beneath him the sea boiled with heavy grey bodies.

'I know yez're here somewhere,' shouted Cord. 'Now git yerselves out into the open quick smart, or I'll let go of 'im.'

Goldie stood frozen to the spot. Whatever she did

next, Mouse would die. If she and Toadspit stayed hidden, he would die in the next few seconds. If they showed themselves, he would still die. They would all die – it would just happen a bit later.

In the back of her mind, Frisia whispered, *As long as you are alive, the battle is not lost.*

Goldie nodded. The princess was right. They must save the little boy *now*. As long as he was still alive – as long as they were *all* still alive – there was a skerrick of hope.

She took a deep breath and let the Nothingness slide away. A moment later Toadspit flickered into view close by.

Cord hissed with satisfaction. His pistol swung up to cover them. 'Ya see?' he growled at Smudge. 'No ghosties. Now git that sword.'

Smudge didn't move. 'Let's take 'em back to the city, Cord, and let 'em go. You can tell Harrow they got away.'

'Shut up,' said Cord. 'I've 'ad enough of you. In fact—' he shook Mouse until the little boy whimpered, '—I've 'ad enough of everyone on this ship. I reckon it's time to do the business. And we'll start with this one.'

He shifted his grip on Mouse's arm, as if he was about to push the boy overboard. Goldie took a quick step forward. 'Wait!' she said. 'There's something you should know.'

She had no idea what she was going to say. Toadspit was standing a little way behind her, as helpless as she was. Neither of them could get closer, not without endangering Mouse. She did not know how they could save the little boy, or themselves.

'What?' growled Cord.

Goldie racked her brain. For some reason, she kept thinking about Frisia's sword. But that was lying on the other side of the deck. If one of them tried to grab it, Cord would just shoot them.

There was Bonnie, of course. But what could Bonnie do? She was as helpless as Goldie and Toadspit.

Or was she?

Like a flash of light, Goldie saw herself standing on the docks at Merne, when she was still a princess and Bonnie was Uschi, a girl who longed to go to war with her brother. A girl who was almost as good an archer as Frisia.

'Here, put these in my cabin.'

The sword had come out of the Lie into the real world. *What if Frisia's bow and quiver had done the same?*

Goldie had no way of knowing. Just as she had no way of knowing whether Bonnie and the person hiding in the dinghy would understand what she was about to say. And whether they could act quickly enough.

All she could do was hope. She took another step forward.

'None of yer tricks,' snapped Cord, raising his pistol. The ship rolled from side to side. Mouse clutched the rail with desperate hands.

'I haven't got any tricks left,' said Goldie. Toadspit shifted his feet, and she knew that he had heard the lie in her voice. Behind her back, her hands twitched in fingertalk. *'Be ready!'*

'But if Princess Frisia were here,' she said loudly, *'she'd* have some tricks. *She* was a famous archer.'

'What?' sneered Cord. 'You think that old Lie's gunna save ya? It won't help you a second time, will it, boy?'

He gave Mouse a push, so that the little boy almost fell off the rail. Mouse cried out. His legs scrabbled in mid-air.

Cord laughed.

'If Princess Frisia were here,' Goldie cried quickly, 'she'd shoot that pistol out of your hand!'

She and Toadspit dived for the deck just in time. An arrow whistled over their heads. It hit Cord's pistol full square, knocking it out of his hand. He yelped with surprise – and let go of Mouse.

The little boy clung to the rail, screaming. His legs flailed. The ship rolled. His hands began to slip . . .

Goldie leaped to her feet and flew across the deck faster than she had ever run before. As Mouse slid over the side of the ship, she grabbed his arm and clung to him with all her strength.

Cord was already diving for his pistol. Out of the corner of her eye Goldie saw Toadspit try to beat him to it and knew that he would not make it in time.

Then she heard a shout of rage, and someone burst out of the dinghy and jumped onto Cord's back.

It was Pounce.

Cord fell to the deck under the sudden weight, his hand still grasping for the pistol. He missed, and it slid across the boards towards Goldie. She kicked it into the scuppers.

But the force of that kick loosened her grip on Mouse's arm. He began to slide away from her. 'Toadspit!' she screamed.

Toadspit raced across the deck and grabbed the little boy's other arm. Together, they pulled him up the side of the ship and over the rail to safety. Then they fell onto the wet boards in a heap.

But they could not rest for long. Nearby, Pounce was fighting for his life. He kicked and punched and bit with a ferocious cunning, but Goldie could see that he was no match for Cord. The sharp-faced man was gradually forcing him to the deck.

She saw the sword, still lying where Smudge had thrown it. A part of her yearned to grab it and wield it. A greater part of her felt sick at the thought.

But she had to do something. She stood up and edged towards the sword.

'Hey!' shouted Smudge, and he let go of the tiller. But before he could reach Goldie, Morg dropped from the clouds. Smudge screamed with fright and fell flat on his face, covering his head with his hands. The slaughterbird stalked around him, jabbing at him with her beak.

Goldie heard a cry from Mouse. Cord was kneeling over Pounce with his arm wrapped around the boy's neck. Pounce wriggled and kicked, but he could not get away, and his face was slowly turning blue.

Toadspit took an uncertain step towards him. Goldie gritted her teeth and reached for the sword.

But as she did so, she felt a rush of wings, and Morg flew up into the rigging. Goldie hesitated, her fingers an inch from the sword's hilt. Above her head, the slaughterbird began to raise and lower her great wings.

Flap. Flap-flap. Flap.

There was a sudden stillness on the deck. The wind and the waves dropped away to nothing. The clouds were so low that they touched the top of the mast. The only sound, apart from the throb of the engine, was Morg's wings, beating out the rhythm of an ancient song.

Flap. Flap-flap. Flap.
Flap. Flap-flap. Flap.

The air around the *Piglet* flickered. Cord grunted. Then he let go of Pounce and staggered to his feet. The movement seemed to make him dizzy. He leaned against the rail, holding his fists out in front of him.

'I'm gunna kill yez all,' he growled.

Smudge sat up, keeping a careful eye on Morg. Pounce rubbed his neck. Goldie heard a whisper of sound, and the cat brushed past her, its gaze as cold as the winter moon. The mice followed it, and formed a semicircle around Cord. Despite their small size, there was something pitiless about them, as if they had made a judgement and were there to see it carried out.

The air fizzed and swirled around them.

It's a Big Lie, thought Goldie. *Morg has summoned a Big Lie!*

Above her head the slaughterbird's wings kept up a steady rhythm. The clouds drifted lower, until they nearly touched the deck.

Cord drew in a sharp breath. 'Oho, so it's you, is it, Bungle?' he muttered. He jabbed at the clouds with his fists. 'Come on then. Come and get yer face rearranged.'

Bonnie's voice breathed in Goldie's ear. 'Who's he talking to?'

'I don't know,' whispered Goldie. The air flickered again, and the clouds took on the outline of a man.

'You was always a weakling, Bungle,' said Cord. 'Weak and slow.' He laughed. 'Not like me.'

Smudge dragged himself to his feet, keeping well away from the cat and mice. 'Cord? Whatcha doin'? Bungle's dead. Ya slit 'is throat five years ago.'

Cord didn't hear him. 'Ya can't fool me, Bungle,' he cried. 'I see ya!' And he lashed out again with his fists.

Goldie stared at the cat and the mice. One of them must have asked a question. *What was it?* she wondered.

Frisia's whisper came as sharp as salt spray in the back of her mind. *When will this man pay for his crimes?*

Goldie shivered. And the answer?

Now . . .

Suddenly Cord's dizziness seemed to leave him. With all his old sureness, he jumped up onto the *Piglet*'s rail. He wrapped one arm around the rigging and threw his head back. 'Ya think ya can git away from me?' he bellowed. 'No one gits away from Cord. I'm comin' after ya, Bungle!'

Smudge stared at him in alarm. 'Watcha doin', Cord? Don't forget the sharks! Cord? The *sharks*!'

But Cord did not hear him. He didn't seem to hear anything, except perhaps the voice of a vengeful ghost in his head. With a fierce shout, he leaped overboard.

For a moment Goldie almost thought he might survive. He swam across the very tops of the waves, barely touching the water. There was no sign of the sharks.

But then he stopped, as if he had hit an invisible wall. The water around him boiled. He gave one single desperate cry.

And was gone.

FIFTH KEEPER

N o one moved for a long
time. The *Piglet* drifted.
The clouds frayed and
blew away. Goldie thought she might
cry, and then she thought she might
laugh, and then she clamped her lips
together and did her best to
think nothing at all.

The bluebird brooch

Toadspit's face was blank;
his arm was tight around
Bonnie's shoulders. Mouse crouched on the deck
behind them, shivering, while his little pets cleaned
his face and groomed his hair, trying to comfort him.

Smudge stared at the horizon, his eyes wide with horror.

It was Pounce who jolted them out of their shock. He strolled to the rail and spat loudly into the water. 'Good riddance to bad rubbish, that's what I say. Hey, Smudge, any of them pastries left? I didn't get no breakfast this mornin'.'

Smudge blinked at him. 'Ya— Ya can't 'ave 'em. They're Cord's. He don't like no one takin' his stuff.'

'Don't reckon he'll be needin' 'em,' said Pounce. He grinned at the cat, which was sitting beside the rail with a satisfied look on its face. 'Don't reckon he'll be needin' this boat, neither. I could sail up and down the Southern Archipelago and make me fortune. Cap'n Pounce. How does that sound?'

He tilted his head in a challenge and stared around the circle of faces. Slowly Goldie's mind started working again. 'It sounds fine,' she said, 'as long as you take us home first.'

Pounce's eyes narrowed. 'It'll cost ya.'

'We've already paid,' said Goldie. She nodded towards Mouse. The white-haired boy was still shivering, but now he crooned to his mice as they trotted up and down his arms.

Pounce flushed. 'Yeah, I s'pose ya have.'

Toadspit shook himself as if he had only just noticed

what was going on. 'You're not going to trust him, are you?' he muttered to Goldie.

'No,' said Goldie, not bothering to lower her voice. 'He'd still sell us to Harrow if it suited him, wouldn't you, Pounce?'

Pounce shrugged. 'Maybe. But I pays me debts too. Ya saved Mousie from the sharks. So I'll give yez a ride 'ome in me ship.'

Toadspit bristled. 'Who says it's your ship?'

'*I* says.'

'I bet you can't even sail it.'

'Can *you?*' said Pounce.

Bonnie had been listening to all this with Frisia's bow held loosely by her side. Now she rolled her eyes at Pounce. 'Of course he can. My brother can do anything.'

'Shut up, Bonnie,' mumbled Toadspit.

'Listen,' said Goldie, losing patience with all of them. 'None of us know how to sail this ship except for Smudge. So it doesn't matter who calls themselves captain. It's going to be Smudge telling us what to do.'

The big man shook his head. 'Not me. I'm not gunna help yez. Harrow wouldn't like it.' Behind him, the cat stretched and showed its claws.

'Harrow won't know,' said Goldie.

Smudge glanced nervously over his shoulder at the cat. He lowered his voice. 'Harrow knows everything.'

'You can be captain,' said Goldie.

Smudge hesitated, and Goldie could see the temptation working away inside him. But his fear of Harrow was too great. He shook his head again.

Goldie sighed loudly. 'In that case we'll just have to *make* you help us.'

'Make me?' Smudge laughed uncertainly. 'How ya gunna do that? Yez are only little. An' I'm big.'

Goldie turned her back on him and winked at Bonnie. 'How many arrows have you got?'

'Lots. Do you want me to shoot him?' said Bonnie. She was only wearing one shoe, and now she kicked it off and stood eagerly in her stockinged feet.

'Hey!' said Smudge.

'Not all at once,' said Goldie. 'Just a bit here and there. Start with his kidneys.'

Bonnie took an arrow from her quiver and fitted it to the bow.

'Hang on a minute,' said Smudge.

Bonnie raised the bow and began to circle the big man. 'Where are his kidneys?'

'I'm not sure,' said Goldie. 'There, I think.' She poked Smudge in the back. 'It doesn't really matter. Just keep trying until you hit them.'

'All right, all right!' said Smudge. 'I'll help yez.'

Bonnie made a disappointed face. 'Can I shoot him anyway?'

'Only if he doesn't get the ship on course for Jewel right now,' said Goldie.

Smudge ran to the tiller, and the *Piglet* was soon heading steadily westward. Goldie sank to the deck and closed her eyes, trying very hard not to think about Cord.

Instead, for the first time in days, she let her thoughts turn to Ma and Pa. How she longed to see them! She wished she could make the ship move more quickly—

'Goldie.'

Reluctantly she opened her eyes. Bonnie and Toadspit were squatting in front of her, with Frisia's bow and sword in their hands. Bonnie must have retrieved her own bow from the dinghy, because she held that as well. Morg sat on Toadspit's shoulder, her black feathers rustling in the wind.

'Ffffowl,' muttered the cat in a half-hearted fashion, from its spot near the rail.

Without a word, Bonnie laid the two bows on the deck. They were the same length, but apart from that they looked nothing at all alike. Frisia's bow was almost new. It had a leather grip, with a small carving of a wolf cub just above it, and it was painted in intricate patterns of red and black. The tips were inlaid with silver rings.

In contrast, Bonnie's bow was so old that it had surely forgotten it had ever been part of a living tree. The original grip was missing, and there were scrapes and scratches all over the wood. If it had ever been painted, there was no sign of it now.

But then Bonnie pointed to the tip, where the bowstring looped around it, and said, 'Look. You can see where the silver rings used to be. And here, just above the grip. It's the wolf cub.'

Goldie peered at the old bow without touching it. Certainly there had once been *something* carved there. But it had been hacked away with a knife long ago, and she could not tell what it was.

'Toadspit reckons I'm imagining things,' said Bonnie.

'I didn't say that,' grinned Toadspit. 'I said you were mad.'

'Well, I'm not. The two bows *feel* the same, Goldie. They really do.'

'I suppose it's possible,' said Goldie slowly. 'Frisia's bow *could* have ended up in the museum somehow.'

'And Olga Ciavolga kept it safe and gave it to me!'

'Which makes Olga Ciavolga the mad one,' said Toadspit. Then he added quickly, 'But don't tell her I said so.'

Bonnie picked up the beautiful new bow. Her fingers

caressed the leather grip. 'Were we really there, in ancient Merne?'

'I don't know,' said Goldie. 'It felt as if we were.'

Over by the rail, the cat inspected a paw that had once been adorned with velvet and rat-skins. 'Ggggown,' it murmured.

Bonnie sighed. 'It was fun being the Young Margravine. And Goldie, you were a good Frisia. Much better than I would've been.'

She stroked the bow one last time, then held it out. 'This is really yours.'

Toadspit cleared his throat. 'This is yours too.' His hand lingered on the hilt of Frisia's sword, as if he didn't want to let it go.

'Yo-o-o-o-urs,' croaked Morg.

Goldie sat up. The silver rings on the bow winked at her. The sword lay still and waiting. Her fingers clenched. 'Um— I've forgotten how to use them.'

She saw the beginnings of disbelief on Toadspit's face, and hurried on. 'I lost the skill when the Big Lie stopped. I don't know why. It just went. You may as well keep them.'

The cat gazed at her, its eyes dark and knowing.

'I haven't forgotten,' said Bonnie.

Toadspit laughed. 'We saw that.' Then his face grew serious again. 'I haven't forgotten either. It doesn't seem fair.'

Goldie forced a smile. 'I don't mind. Really.'

She was glad when they snatched the weapons up and carried them away. She was glad too when the cat fell asleep on a coil of rope. She wished *she* could sleep, but she was wide awake now.

It wasn't easy to fool Toadspit. She had only been able to do it because he wanted the sword so much. She *hadn't* forgotten how to use it. She hadn't forgotten a thing that had happened during the Big Lie. Her hands and mind and heart remembered every skilful movement of sword and bow.

Even now a part of her wanted to jump up and snatch the weapons away from her friends. To wrap her fingers around the hilt of the sword, and feel that glorious weight in her hand . . .

Frisia.

The Lie had ended, but the princess's voice was still there inside her. And so was her love of war and fighting.

Goldie gritted her teeth. There were things she admired about the princess, but the love of war was not one of them. As far as *she* could see, the main thing that happened in war was that ordinary people had their lives torn apart for no good reason.

But Frisia's fate-telling had been meant for her as well, she knew that now. The fire was the Fugleman.

The household that he threatened to destroy was Jewel. And she must not hold back.

The trouble was, the princess's love of war wasn't the only thing that she carried hidden inside her. The wolf-sark was there too, ready to blaze up as soon as she drew the sword. She had nearly killed Mouse because of it. Who might she kill if it happened again?

She shuddered. It was better to give her weapons away.

'Hey, Princess,' shouted Smudge, interrupting her thoughts. 'Am I really the captain, like you said?'

He had been holding the tiller on a steady course for some time, and had apparently accepted what had happened. But Goldie knew they would have to watch him. Just as they would have to watch Pounce. She would not let herself be betrayed again.

'I'm not a princess,' she shouted.

'What are ya then? *Who* are ya?'

Goldie drew in a long breath. She didn't know what they would find when they reached Jewel, but if Guardian Hope had told the truth about the mercenaries, it seemed likely that there would be a war of one sort or another. And she and Toadspit and Bonnie would be caught up in it.

She would not glory in it, like Frisia did. She would not wield a sword or a bow if she could possibly help it.

But neither would she hold back. She would fight the Fugleman in her own way, and with all her strength.

Who was she? What was she? She wrapped her fingers around her bird brooch. There was only one possible answer.

'I'm Goldie Roth,' she cried. 'I'm Fifth Keeper of the Museum of Dunt!'

Meanwhile, back in Jewel . . . the Fugleman was being unchained from the desk for the last time. His guards, of course, did not know that it was the last time. He took care not to let them see the smile of anticipation that flickered across his face.

They were not smiling. There had been no further messages from Spoke, and it was clear that something had gone wrong with the rescue. The children were lost, perhaps even dead. The guards muttered among themselves, trying to decide who was responsible.

They blamed the mysterious Harrow. With a little encouragement from the Fugleman, they blamed the

Protector. They blamed everyone except the Fugleman himself.

Which was exactly as it should be.

When the first shots sounded in the distance, they almost fell over with astonishment. The Fugleman could see it on their faces. *Gunfire?* In *Jewel?*

'Don't mind me,' he murmured. 'I'm sure it is your duty to go and see what is happening. Just lock me in my cell and I'll be here when you return.'

They did as he told them, fools that they were. He waited until he could no longer hear their voices, then he strode to the middle of the cell and, for the first time in days, drew himself up to his full height. The mask of false humility fell away. He raised his fists in the air – and laughed. He was the Fugleman, the leader of the Blessed Guardians and spokesman for the Seven Gods!

Soon his mercenaries would fight their way to his side. The moment they freed him, he would go and visit his *dear* sister.

He laughed again, glorying in the thought of what was to come. This was surely the end for the Protector! But for him it was just the beginning . . .

ACKNOWLEDGEMENTS

Many thanks once again to Peter Matheson for his invaluable feedback on the various drafts of *City of Lies* – and for the idea that Frisia's sword might come out the other end of a Big Lie.

Thanks to the talented and enthusiastic people at Allen & Unwin Children's Books, particularly Eva Mills and Susannah Chambers for their clear and brilliant editing, but also to Emmeline Goodchild, Jyy-Wei Ip, Julia Imogen, Katy McEwen and Angela Namoi for their hard work on behalf of The Keepers Trilogy.

Design by Committee and Sebastian Ciaffaglione have created another beautiful cover for this book, and Sebastian's character illustrations give Goldie, her friends and enemies an extra dimension.

And finally, I am indebted as always to my agent Margaret Connolly for her expertise, her enthusiasm and her support in times of creeping doubt.

ABOUT THE AUTHOR

LIAN TANNER is a children's author and playwright. She has worked as a teacher in Australia and Papua New Guinea, as well as a tourist-bus driver, a freelance journalist, a juggler, a community arts worker, an editor and a professional actor. It took her a while to realise that all of these jobs were really just preparation for being a writer. Nowadays she lives by the beach in southern Tasmania, with a small tabby cat and lots of friendly neighbourhood dogs. She has not yet mastered the art of Concealment by the Imitation of Nothingness, but she is quite good at Camouflage.

Turn the page
for a sneak preview of
the stunning final book...

THE KEEPERS

PATH of BEASTS

THE CAPTIVE CITY

It was night-time when the three children entered the city of Jewel. Ragged and filthy, they clung to the shadows, their feet making no sound on the cobbled paths.

They had been gone for weeks, torn away from home without the chance to say goodbye, and they were bursting with impatience to see their parents. But they carried secrets with them – secrets that would get them killed if they were caught by the

Goldie Roth

wrong people. And so they stopped and listened at every corner.

They saw no one, but the hair on the backs of their necks prickled and their faces were pale with tension. This was not the city they had left behind. Fear hung over the streets, as thick as fog. The light of the watergas lamps seemed to tremble as it spilled across the deserted footpaths. The houses, with their locked doors and tightly drawn curtains, held their breath.

The children crept deeper and deeper into the city, until at last they came to the Bridge of Beasts, where it crossed the Grand Canal. They paused there, watching for any sign of movement. Then they slipped across the bridge one by one.

They were close to their homes now, and eager to press on. But the last few weeks had taught them the value of caution, and they paused again.

It was just as well they did. Somewhere nearby a boot struck the cobblestones. Immediately, Goldie gave a hand signal and all three children pressed into the shadows at the end of the bridge. Toadspit wrapped his fingers around the hilt of the sword that he carried at his side. His younger sister Bonnie gripped her longbow. But Goldie shook her head fiercely at them, and they did not move again.

The five men who came swaggering up the middle

of the boulevard were clearly soldiers, although their uniforms and haversacks seemed to be made up of bits and pieces from a dozen different armies. They carried rifles slung across their chests, and their eyes and teeth gleamed in the gaslight. They looked as if they owned the city and everything in it.

Goldie had been expecting something like this, but still it was a shock to see such men on the streets of Jewel. She found her hand straying towards the sword on Toadspit's hip. Her breath quickened . . .

No! She jerked her hand back. The wolf-sark, the battle madness that she carried so unwillingly inside her, lay just below the surface. If she drew that sword she would be lost. She had almost killed someone last time the wolf-sark took hold of her. She would not risk it happening again.

She swallowed her anger and prayed that the soldiers would pass quickly.

But the soldiers seemed to have no intention of passing. One of them, a tall man with red side-whiskers that curled almost to his chin, leaned his rifle against the canal fence and took biscuits and a water canteen from his haversack. His companions copied him.

Toadspit touched Goldie's hand, tapping out a question in the quick, subtle movements of fingertalk. '*Go or stay?*'

Goldie chewed her lip. She and Toadspit could easily slip away without being seen. If they *really* wanted to, they could probably steal the biscuits out of the soldiers' hands and leave them wondering where their supper had gone. But Bonnie had not had the same training and might well be spotted.

'*Stay,*' Goldie signed.

The men lounged against the fence, throwing biscuits at each other and guffawing at the tops of their voices, as if they wanted everyone in the surrounding houses to hear them and tremble. They reminded Goldie of the soldiers she and Toadspit had encountered deep inside the Museum of Dunt, behind the Dirty Gate. *Those* soldiers were the remnants of an ancient war that only survived within the museum. They carried pikes and swords and old-fashioned muskets, and spoke in the accents of Old Merne.

But these men were modern, and their scrappy uniforms suggested that they were mercenaries, whose loyalty could be bought and sold. Goldie wondered what they had done with the city's militia. And where was the Grand Protector? *She* would never have allowed mercenaries on the streets of Jewel—

Goldie's thoughts were interrupted by the sound of a street-rig clattering over cobblestones. The mercenaries

4

hastily shovelled food and drinks back into their haversacks and grabbed their rifles.

'What sort of idiot drives around after curfew?' growled the red-haired man. 'Anyone'd think they *want* to be stuck in the House of Repentance!'

'They're coming this way,' said one of his companions, strutting out into the middle of the road.

Spoked wheels rattled towards him. An engine roared, and headlights pierced the shadows that surrounded the children. Goldie dared not look at her friends, but she could feel Bonnie as tense as a wire beside her, and Toadspit, balanced on the balls of his feet, ready to run. If the mercenaries turned around now . . .

But the men were strung across the boulevard, blocking the path of the approaching street-rig. For a moment, Goldie thought it wasn't going to stop. It rumbled towards the soldiers at a steady pace, bathing them in light. Its horn blared twice. An angry voice shouted something incoherent. The mercenaries raised their rifles and took careful aim at the cabin behind the lights.

With a squeal of brakes, the street-rig skidded to a halt. The engine died. The shout came again, but this time Goldie heard it clearly.

'How dare you? How *dare* you? Remove yourselves from our path immediately!'

The mercenaries didn't budge. 'Out of the rig,' said the red-haired man in a bored tone. 'Come on, make it quick.'

There was a mutter of voices and, to Goldie's relief, the headlights snapped off. By the time her eyes had adjusted, two people were stepping down from the street-rig – two people wearing the heavy black robes and black boxy hats of the Blessed Guardians.

A shiver of loathing ran through Goldie. It was more than six months since the Blessed Guardians had been banished from the city. The Grand Protector had put them on trial first, for treason and cruelty. Then she had thrown every single one of them out of Jewel, with a warning never to return.

But here they were, back again.

Goldie touched Toadspit's hand. '*Leave now, while they're busy,*' she signed.

Toadspit nodded, and murmured in his sister's ear. But before they could move, the two Guardians swept past the mercenaries and marched straight towards the end of the bridge.

'Hey!' shouted the red-haired man, striding after them with his side-whiskers bristling. 'Where do you think you're going? There's supposed to be no one on the streets at night. That's our orders.'

The Blessed Guardians stopped, not five paces from

where the children crouched. One of them, a man with very pale skin, raised his eyebrows. 'The curfew doesn't apply to *us*, you fool!' he said, in a high, grating voice. 'Go and carry out your orders somewhere else.'

He turned to his companion, as if the mercenaries had already gone, and waved his hand at the canal. 'This place will do as well as anywhere. It is tidal here, and the levees are open. The – ah – rubbish will be swept out to sea before morning.'

'But what if it is not?' said the second Guardian, a woman, in worried tones. 'If someone sees it, it could cause trouble.'

Goldie's heart pounded against her ribs, and her fingers crept to the blue bird brooch that was pinned inside her collar. The Guardians had only to turn their heads, and she and her friends would be discovered.

'If someone *sees* it,' said the pale man, 'we will simply convince them that they did *not* see it.' He laughed. 'And if they persist in their error, well then, I believe there are still plenty of empty cells in the House of Repentance.'

Behind him, the mercenaries muttered to each other. The red-haired man clearly resented being called a fool and, when the Guardians turned to walk back to their street-rig, he blocked their path.

'The way *I* understand it,' he said, 'no one on the streets means *no one* on the streets. Nothing in our orders about making an exception for people in funny hats.'

His friends sniggered. The pale man sighed, and spoke slowly, as if he was dealing with very small children. 'Listen carefully. I am Guardian Kindness, and this—' he nodded to the woman at his side '—is Guardian Meek. We are here on the Fugleman's business. Remember the Fugleman?' His voice was sarcastic. 'He is our leader. He is also the Lord High Protector of this city. Which means that, while you are in his employ, he is *your* leader as well.'

Goldie felt Bonnie's cold hand slip into hers, and knew that they were all wondering the same thing. If the Fugleman, the worst traitor in the history of Jewel, was truly in charge, and calling himself Protector, what had happened to the real Protector?

'It would not be wise,' continued Guardian Kindness, 'to hinder us. In fact, you would do better to help. We have a certain parcel that we need to dispose of. Please get it out of the rig and bring it here.'

The red-haired man snorted. 'You want us to do your work for you? I don't think so!' He began to walk away. The other mercenaries followed.

'You *will* bring it here, if you know what's good for you. We are the servants of the Seven Gods and they will not be kind to those who oppose us.'

Something in Guardian Kindness's high voice made Goldie's skin crawl. She flicked her fingers to ward off the attentions of the Seven Gods. So did the red-haired man. But he kept walking.

The youngest of the mercenaries, however, hesitated. 'What sort of parcel?'

'It is just some rubbish that we wish to dispose of,' said Guardian Meek quickly. 'It won't take a minute to throw it in the canal. A strong fellow like you—'

'Leave it!' snapped the red-haired man, over his shoulder. 'It's their business, not ours. We're not taking orders from *them*!'

'It is apparent,' said Guardian Kindness, 'that you do not understand your proper place—'

He was interrupted by the very ordinary sound of a man clearing his throat. It had an immediate effect. The Blessed Guardians snapped to attention. A chill ran up Goldie's spine. She heard the hiss of Toadspit's indrawn breath, and felt Bonnie's nails dig into her hand.

The door of the street-rig swung open. An elegant boot appeared, followed by an immaculate trouser leg. A cloak, blacker than the blackest of nights, fell around that leg in perfect folds. A sword glittered in the lamplight.

It was the Fugleman.